CHOKECHERRY DRIVE

it is hard to judge
I would give it
a six

3.

Print ISBN: 9781795413879

eBook ISBN: B07N2CHLXZ

Cover designer: Steven Novak Illustration

CHOKECHERRY DRIVE

DRIVE

LAYLA REED

ACKNOWLEDGEMENTS

Writing a book has always been a goal of mine. Although I always dreamt of publication, I never actually pictured it happening. It would not have been possible without all of the love, support, and encouragement from each and every one of you.

To Vanessa, Patti, Steph and Julie – thank you for reading this book, finding all of my mistakes, and providing your wonderful feedback. Knowing I can count on all of you made this process so much sweeter.

I would also like to thank my editors, Shelley and Dennis, my formatter, Kari, and my cover designer, Steven.

Last but not least, I would like to thank my husband, Scott, and my two children, Lainey and Wesley. Your encouragement has meant the world to me.

CHAPTER 1

MACY

APRIL 2014
LOS ANGELES, CALIFORNIA

Beep, beep, beep. The second snooze alarm went off. Hitting the snooze a third time would make everyone late, which no one could afford to do today. Groaning reluctantly, I dragged myself out from sleep, dug my way out of the covers, and turned the damn thing off.

"Time to get up, Seth," I yawned. "Today's your big day." Reaching out for Seth, I realized his side of our four-poster King bed was cold. He's already up. I doubt he slept more than a few hours. Seth has been working fourteen to sixteen-hour days for almost a year on his latest celebrity divorce, and this case was finally wrapping up, which was a relief to all of us. Seth promised a family vacation when this was all over, which I plan to take full advantage of.

Slipping on my slippers and robe, I headed down to the girls' room. "Rise and shine girls! Time to get up!" Throwing open their curtains, both girls instinctively covered their eyes from the corners of their twin beds. For some reason I will never understand, the girls chose to share their room. Living in a 4,200 square foot home, there was no shortage of bedrooms,

1

bathrooms, or any other space. My daughters, ages eleven and nine, certainly had their fair share of daily fights, but never once have they ever thought about having their own room. I knew this would come, so I chose to enjoy every minute of this time. Their giggles at night were comforting, and even though I knew I should go in and make them go to bed during those magical moments, I just couldn't do it. Bree and Ella had a sisterly bond that I will never know or understand.

The smell of coffee filled my nostrils as I headed downstairs. Seth was rarely up to start the coffee. He must be beside himself. It was hard to see him so stressed out, but he just shrugged and said, "All this hard work will pay off someday." However, to my surprise, Seth was sitting at the dining room table, dressed in his suit and tie, coffee and paper in hand.

Coming up behind him, I wrapped my arms around his neck and kissed the back of his full head of black hair.

"Mr. Whitaker, you are looking strikingly handsome this morning." Seth grabbed my arms, and in one swift motion, I was sitting on his lap. After fifteen years of marriage, I knew when he needed a little extra support. This was the biggest case of his career to date, and in hours the case *could* settle, which meant we *could* get on with our lives, and Seth *could* be a little less stressed.

"Did you get any sleep?" The slight circles under his dark eyes answered my question, but I still waited to hear it from him.

He shrugged. "Not really."

"Want some breakfast?"

"I had some toast, earlier. I'll be fine. I really need to get to the courtroom before the press gets there."

The conversation was over before it really began. There was no point in starting an argument with Seth, not today, or any other day either. There was always something else, or someone of more importance, some celebrity, who got the most of my husband's attention. There was no sense in ruining his day before it began with a silly fight about breakfast or any other little mundane thing. Sighing, I hopped off his lap and headed to the kitchen for some much-needed coffee of my own, and to start making the girls' breakfast and pack their lunches.

"Macy, where are the keys to the Lincoln?" Seth shouted from the office. He only took the Lincoln out for special occasions. He must have been just as optimistic as I was about this case settling today.

"Top drawer on the right," I yelled back, knowing he probably didn't hear me.

Bree frantically ran into the kitchen. "I can't find my purple sweater. I need my purple sweater, or I will never pass this test," she wailed. Bree, my eleven-year old, has always had the most dramatic and superstitious flair. Today it was the purple sweater; tomorrow it will be something else.

"It's hanging in the laundry room, sweetie," I replied, flipping the pancakes. "Tell Ella that breakfast is ready." Bree stomped off, growling towards the laundry room.

Seth and Ella got to the kitchen at the same time. "I found the keys, Macy; they were in the top drawer." Seth kissed Ella on the forehead. "Wish Daddy luck!"

"Good luck!" Ella and I said together. "Bree's in the laundry room," I answered before Seth asked. Seth never left the house without saying good-bye to his girls. "She needs her purple sweater or she won't pass her test." I mocked her while Seth rolled his eyes. We certainly have been blessed with both of our girls, even with the pre-teen drama. Although Seth would never admit it, I have secretly wondered how much he's wanted a boy.

"I found it," Bree grumbled, coming into the kitchen a few minutes later. Turning her nose up at the pancakes, she grabbed her sack lunch and headed for the door. "Hurry up, Ella, the bus will be here any minute!" Ella hastily gulped down her pancakes, her round freckled face sticky with syrup.

Seth laughed at her sticky face and, briefcase in hand, he blew us all a kiss and left. Without watching, I knew that Seth would stop at the mirror one last time, check his hair and straighten his tie before leaving. He really did seem calmer. I wondered if it was self-assurance or if this case had beaten him down to where he just wanted it to be over with. It was probably both. Never the less, all of our lives would be a lot easier after today. Well, at least until the next case came along.

"Bree, I will pick you up after drama practice today. Good luck on your test. Ella, remember Mrs. Smith will be here after school for piano practice," I said, hugging them on their way out the door. Ella turned to wave one last time before she started jogging towards her sister, who was almost to the bus.

Sighing, I made a mental list of all the things I needed to do. First on the list was tidying up the kitchen, then working out, go tanning, stop at the dry cleaners, the post office and supermarket, come home to start supper, and get Bree from drama practice. Even with a housekeeper, I found I could hardly get everything done that I needed to.

We hired Elvira, our housekeeper, when Bree was two. She was a Godsend and we all love her dearly. She did everything from watching the kids, to dusting, laundry, meals and she kept up on my flower beds. I used to do all of our yard work, until one summer the paparazzi caught me bending over in my flower garden. The picture was less than flattering, and thankfully it resulted in nothing. It never got published, but it left me uneasy and self-conscious. After each celebrity court case, Seth was followed by the paparazzi for a short time. It seemed to die down fast, but during that time I always worried about my appearance.

"It's good for business," Seth always brushed it off. But after that picture of me, bending over in neon green leggings, my rolls bursting out the sides of my too tight black tank top, drenched in sweat, Seth was a little more willing to consider other options. He had a privacy fence put in, and hired Elvira. As for me, I worked out six days a week ever since. That picture became my best motivation.

Although I never actually saw the photo, I had a pretty good idea of what it looked like. So, my personal trainer came at least three days a week, and I visited the gym at least three days a week. And I also always made sure I looked my best when I went out, especially when out with Seth, so that I did not embarrass him. My husband scoffed at my insecurities, calling me ridiculous. But his appreciative eyes told me all I needed to know.

By the time I got out of the shower, post workout, I heard the television blaring in the kitchen downstairs. Elvira always had the radio or television on while she worked, and it was always much louder than it needed to be. I was just about to start with my make-up, when Elvira came flying through my bedroom, right into my bathroom.

"Senora! Senora Whitaker!" Elvira panted.

Startled, I poked my eye with my eye shadow

brush. "Elvira, what's wrong? Are you okay?" I asked, grabbing her arm. She had never barged in on me in the bathroom like this.

"Come quick!" she gasped. "Senor Whitaker is on the TV!"

I pushed past Elvira and ran down the stairs into the kitchen. Elvira was trying to catch up, but I was not willing to wait. Not today. This was the biggest case of Seth's career. I should have just turned on the television in our bedroom and watched there. Instead, I just followed the noise coming from the kitchen. For once the extra loud volume coming from the TV didn't bother me.

The television screen showed the court house steps with news crews everywhere. Bodyguards were waiting by the entrance for my husband and his client to exit the building. I started biting my nails while Elvira huffed and puffed next to me.

"Reporting live from CNN, I'm Victoria Giant. We have just received word that Augustus and Asia Prescott have reached a settlement agreement and that their divorce is now final. The two actors have a net worth of $450 million, including a home in Beverly Hills, a home in the Hamptons, and a condo in New York City. A private jet, three classic cars, and a ski lodge in Colorado were just a few of the couple's assets that will need to be divided. And let's not forget their dog that they saved from a puppy mill, their boxer named Roxie."

"The couple met and fell in love on the movie set 'Don't Make Me Choose.' The pair wed three months after they first met in Oahu, Hawaii. Their marriage lasted only three and a half years. This was Augustus' first marriage, and Asia's second. Augustus has a child from a previous relationship. The pair never had children together. Oh, here they come now!"

Camera crews and photographers invaded the steps as Seth walked out arm in arm with his client, Asia Prescott. The bodyguards engulfed them as they tried to make their way down the steps, where a podium was waiting. The press wasn't giving them much space, and cameras were flashing directly in their faces.

Asia looked absolutely stunning. She was wearing a strapless red dress, and her large, perky breasts were about to pop out of the top. I'm not really sure how she tucked in those nipples. Her dress had a slit all the way up to her hip bone, revealing her tanned, toned, lean legs. She was wearing black stilettos. I could barely wear high-heels. Her red hair was pulled back in a bun. If you could have torn your eyes off her breasts and up to her face, you would have seen her full, pouty, luscious red lips. I'm not sure what it was you injected to get those lips to look like that, nor would I want to. Never-the-less, she looked like she could be walking on the red carpet if she weren't wearing dark sun glasses, looking somber.

Asia Prescott didn't remove her large sun glasses even as she and Seth reached the podium. Asia was clinging to Seth's shoulder as if he was her life-line. The reporters started shouting questions at them as Seth adjusted the microphone. I slowly exhaled, not realizing I'd been holding my breath.

"Please respect my client's wishes for privacy during this difficult time. Mr. Prescott and my client have reached a confidential settlement of all their assets. Their divorce is now final. The divorce was a mutual decision from both Mr. Prescott and my client. No third parties were involved. My client wishes nothing but the best for Mr. Prescott and all his future endeavors. They have much love and respect for each other and will remain close friends. We consider the matter closed and will not be taking any questions at this time. Thank you."

The bodyguards immediately closed around the two and tried to maneuver them down the last remaining flight of stairs. Cameras were still flashing, and the press started shouting questions at them. *Who got the dog? Is there shared custody? Will they ever make another film together? Are they going to sell the ski lodge? Did you take him for everything he's worth? What can we expect from Asia Prescott in the future?* When Seth and Asia got to the waiting limousine, Seth let her in first, guiding her gracefully so she didn't flash the cameras. The press surrounded the limo as they slowly pulled away. Footage went back to the news anchor, who was ready to re-cap the couple's history and what little they knew of the divorce outcome.

What a relief! This case was finally over. Seth must have been as elated as I was. He would spend the next several weeks wrapping things up, probably traveling and making public appearances with Asia. He usually satin the audience, nodding his approval of things she could talk about and intervening when there were questions she should not answer. He has made appearances on *Good Morning America, Dr. Phil, Entertainment Tonight, 20/20,* and *The View.* This was wonderful publicity and most likely he will have dozens of voicemails waiting at his office. And the cycle will start all over again. But, not before I got our promised vacation.

Elvira went back to cleaning the kitchen, while I mentally started planning our trip. New York City would be a good place to take the girls, or maybe, a cruise. Even a trip back to Myrtle Beach would be fun. Maybe the girls could decide this time and surprise us both.

My ringing cell phone jerked me back to the present. Seth couldn't be calling already. I glanced at the phone number, recognizing it immediately.

"Hello?"

"Mrs. Whitaker, this is Sandy calling from the Long Prairie Nursing home."

"Oh yes, Sandy. Is there something wrong with the payment? My accountant has assured us that everything is up to date."

"Oh certainly, Mrs. Whitaker. This call is not in regards to any payments. The reason for my call is, um…" Sandy paused.

"Yes?" The hairs stood up on the back of my neck. I knew I was not going to like what she was about to say.

"I'm, um, I'm afraid that Mr. Reilly's health has steadily declined in the past week. It's – it's…I think it's time that we discuss Hospice."

Chapter 2

Macy

"Hospice?" I managed to squeak after what felt like an eternity.

"I'm so, so sorry, Mrs. Whitaker. We have notified Mr. Reilly, er, Brandon Reilly of his latest condition. Would you like to arrange for a time for us to meet to go over this? I know this must come as a shock."

"Um, yes, yes it is. What happened to my Dad? When? Why wasn't I notified earlier?" I couldn't seem to stop blubbering.

"About a week ago, Mr. Reilly—" Sandy started to respond, but the in-coming call cut her off. I glanced down at my phone. My brother Brandon was calling.

"I'm sorry Sandy, my brother is on the line. I will start making arrangements with him and I will be there as soon as I can." I didn't give her time to respond and I hit the call waiting button. "Brandon?"

"Hi Macy. I just got a call from the nursing home. Dad's not doing so well."

"I know, they were just on the other line. Sandy said they need to sit down with us to talk about Hospice. I will get the next available flight out." My

10

mind raced.

"Macy, you don't have to come right away. I could meet with them and let you know what's going on. I know you and Seth are really busy. We saw Seth on the news with that movie star."

"No, I want to be there," I insisted.

There was a long pause on the other end. "Are you sure?" Brandon asked, slowly. For the third time today, I froze in my tracks.

"I'm sure." I replied curtly.

"Ok," Brandon responded, almost apologetically. "Charlotte insists that you stay here. You can stay in Nana's cabin. Stay as long as you need to."

"Fine," I said, knowing that that was the least of my worries. "I will text you my flight details when I have them."

My Dad. Hospice. I was almost certain when we placed him in the nursing home that he didn't even need to be there. Up until a year ago, he was living in Nana's cabin and I thought he was doing well. Yes, he had had several falls and was using his walker, but Brandon was right there if he needed anything. However, I understood that this was an added responsibility that Brandon didn't need. Charlotte was almost nine months pregnant with their fourth child at that time, and Brandon was doing his best to keep the farm afloat. Running Dad to his doctor appointments, running all his other errands besides, and checking on him several times a day was taking its toll on Brandon. So, I made a few calls, and once they got an opening, my Dad moved in. Paying for his care was the least I could do as I was never close enough to help out.

The nursing home was the best thing we could have done for him, although it didn't feel like it at the time. For the first time since Mom had died, Dad actually seemed happy, even though he refused to admit it. He spent hours playing cards and working on puzzles in their game room. They had monthly casino trips, movie dates, and he spent a lot of time flirting with the ladies. I received monthly emails on his activities, as well as updates from his doctors. There were times when we would call, and he would be too busy to answer. Yet here we were, one year later, discussing Hospice.

Seth's phone went straight to voicemail – twice. The law firm would more than likely be celebrating long into the night. As much as I hated to put a damper on his fun, he had to know. This could end up changing all of Seth's appearances for the next week. Would they send another lawyer in his place? The timing couldn't have been worse. I called Seth's assistant and asked her to get me the next one-way flight out to Minneapolis and a rental car, too.

What next? Pack, I needed to pack. I ran upstairs into my room and was surprised to find Elvira already in there, unzipping my luggage.

"Oh, Elvira," I said, giving her a big hug. "What would I do without you?"

"Never mind that, Senora Whitaker. I will stay and watch the girls. For as long as you need me."

"Oh Elvira, I couldn't possibly ask that of you. I have no idea how long I will be gone. It could be a week or two. And I'm not sure if I will stay until my Dad, umm…" I couldn't finish that statement, there was a lump in my throat. *My Dad was dying.*

"There is no one else to watch the girls. I know their schedules. Senor Whitaker is very busy. You go. I stay. Bree and Ella will not miss anything here. Now pack."

Elvira was absolutely right. She ran our household

and knew our schedules better than we did. My daughters adored her. They loved spending time with her and they have always whined for her whenever she was on vacation, which was rare. But that's not all she was right about. We really had no one else.

***

Four hours later I sat in first class, waiting for the rest of the passengers to board. I still hadn't heard from Seth, everything was going straight to voicemail. I didn't know how to tell him that my Father was going into Hospice, and that when I saw him next, he might not even know me. It could very well be the last time I saw my Dad alive, if I made it home on time.

Thankfully I got a window seat. The aisle seat was still empty, and I was crossing my sweaty fingers that it stayed that way. For almost four hours my phone would be turned off, so I tried to make one last ditch effort to call Seth. It rang just as my aisle seat passenger plopped down, laden with several bags.

"Hey baby!" Seth shouted. There was loud cheering, clapping and music in the background.

"Seth! Where are you?" I covered my mouth and talked as loudly as I could without disrupting other passengers.

"What baby? I can't hear you!" Seth shouted again.

Embarrassed, I hung up the phone and texted him instead. *Heading to Grey Eagle, Dad needs me. Call when you can.* I quickly turned off my phone and shoved it in my purse as my airline companion struggled to get her bags under her seat.

"Oh my," she huffed, pulling out several magazines. One of the magazines featured Asia and Augustus Prescott on their wedding day, looking radiant, standing under an arch of lilies and orchids in

Oahu. The caption on the tabloid read *"Divorce showdown! A settlement expected soon!"*

"I guess money can't buy happiness," she sighed as she shoved the magazine towards me. I only nodded as I turned on the fan. The cold air came bursting out as I tried to take some deep breaths. As the plane doors closed, my chest started to get tighter, my heart pounded in my ears, and my palms started sweating. *Inhale, exhale. Inhale, exhale.* There was no way to survive this plane ride, or this trip, without my bottle of Ativan.

"Flight jitters?" the heavyset woman asked as I shakily ransacked my bag, looking for my pills. I was shaking so much that it was a miracle that I didn't lose anything.

"Something like that," I muttered back, annoyed that she didn't notice I was trying to avoid conversation.

"Are you flyin' for business or pleasure?"

"Neither." That same lump in my throat came back so I grabbed a neck pillow and closed my eyes. As much as I hated meaningless conversations with strangers, as much as I hated plane rides, and as much as I hated going home to see my Father (most likely for the last time), none of those were reasons for this full-blown panic attack. It was much, much more than that. It was going back to the farm on Chokecherry Drive, the place that had haunted me every day for the last twenty years. It was time to face the ghosts that I had buried in my heart and in my mind, whether I was ready to or not. But would I come out of it unscathed? Would anyone?

***

It was late by the time the flight had landed and I gathered my luggage and rental car. Seth had called twice and texted. When I tried calling him back, there was no answer. Obviously, he was still celebrating his victory. Elvira was working on homework with Bree and Ella. They were surprised I was gone when they got home, and they had a lot of questions on their Grandfather's condition, all of which I had no answers to. After reassuring the girls I would call as soon as I had any updates, I called Brandon. I wanted to let him know I was going to Long Prairie to see Dad first before heading back to Grey Eagle.

"Do you want me to meet you up there?" he asked.

"No, no that's fine. I just want to stop in to see him tonight." *Alone*, I thought.

"Alright," he answered. "The light will be on in the cabin. Charlotte set it up once we knew you were coming. We might be sleeping before you get back. We have an appointment with Sandy and Hospice after breakfast tomorrow. Goodnight Macy."

Hanging up, I felt a little more relieved that the appointment was set up. Had I not been exhausted by travel, I would have coordinated these meetings. I wasn't quite ready to see my Dad yet, but I also wasn't quite ready to head out to the farm. I needed a little more time, and courage, to gather my thoughts.

The two-hour drive from Minneapolis to Long Prairie did nothing to settle my nerves. Each passing town was familiar, yet somehow foreign. I had only been to Minnesota twice since I left, Brandon and Charlotte's wedding, and my Mother's funeral. Chances were this was last time I would ever return to Minnesota. When my Father did pass, there would be nothing left for me to return to. Brandon and I hardly knew each other anymore. Charlotte and I had never been close, and I was not even sure I knew all of their children's names. There were no family reunions, no holidays to share. Maybe it was because Brandon chose to stay on the family farm. Maybe it was because our worlds were just too far apart and we had nothing in common except our DNA. Or maybe because all I saw was disappointment in Brandon's eyes when he looked at me. He remembered too. And nothing I could do would ever change that.

It was almost 9 p.m. when I pulled into the parking lot. The lot was nearly empty, a sure sign that visiting hours were over. I checked my phone again, confirming that there were no missed calls or voicemails from Seth, made sure my Ativan bottle was still in my purse, and headed for the door.

The waiting area was dark and no one was sitting at the front desk. I had no idea what room my father was staying in. He'd been here for almost a year, and I never bothered to ask. Whenever I would call, I would just ask for Mr. Reilly and they would transfer my call. Instantly, that all too familiar lump in my throat came back. It was one more reminder that I could never, and will never, be the good daughter they so desperately wanted me to be.

There was someone humming from the hallway, so I moved closer to the front desk. "Excuse me?" I called out, hoping that the nurse heard me.

"Be right there!" someone called back. A few minutes later she appeared, looking at me oddly. "Can I help you, Ma'am? All of our residents are settled in for the evening."

"I'm sorry. I just flew in from Los Angeles today, and I came straight here. I know it's really late, but I just really need to see my Father. I'm not sure what room he is in."

The nurse relaxed a little and smiled. "Of course, Ma'am. A few minutes won't hurt. Who is he?"

"Howard Reilly."

She offered me a sympathetic smile and motioned for me to follow her down a long hallway. "Oh, yes, Hun – come with me. He is in room 110. He has been sleeping a lot the past few days, and he hasn't eaten a thing. You must be Mrs. Whitaker?" I nodded. "If you need anything, just holler. My name is Gracie," she continued as she pushed the door open and walked right in.

Dad appeared to be sleeping peacefully even though he was hooked up to IV's. He had aged considerably; his hair was thin and pure white, his discolored skin made it obvious that he didn't have much time left. *How long has it been since I have seen him?*

"Come on in and pull up that chair," Gracie motioned. "Mr. Reilly, your daughter is here to see you. She traveled a very long way today," she said while checking his pulse and pushing buttons on the machine.

My legs finally remembered how to move, and I pulled up a chair next to his bed. There weren't any decorations, pictures or any traces of home anywhere. No animal heads from his years of hunting, no framed pictures or flowers on the night stand. However, right above his night stand was a small tag board, with only two pictures. One was a family snapshot of Brandon, Charlotte, and the kids. The other was a family picture of us from a few years back, from our trip to Boston. *Has it really been that long since I sent him pictures of us?*

"Can I get you anything, Mrs. Whitaker? Can I get you coffee, or water? We also have a vending machine right down the hall."

"No, thank you. I'm - I'm fine right now." My voice cracked and my hands started to shake.

"Mrs. Whitaker, are you all right?"

It took a moment to compose myself. "Do you think he can hear me?" I whispered.

Gracie gave another sympathetic smile and she squeezed my shoulder. "Of course he can, dear. Say what you need to say to him now, while you still have the chance. I am certain he can hear you, even if he can't respond. He knows you're here. I'm sure nothing would make him happier than hearing from you." With another light squeeze, she left the room.

For a while I just sat there concentrating on the slow rise and fall of his chest. I studied his face, contemplating what I wanted, no needed, to say to my Father. So many emotions came flooding back, and before I could even reach for another Ativan, I choked out a sob. I grabbed his hand, pressed it firmly against my cheek, and I cried. "Oh, Daddy, I'm so, so sorry for everything that happened. It's entirely my fault. I'm so sorry I wasn't here, I'm so sorry that I couldn't be here. It was just too…too hard. And that was just incredibly selfish of me, and now I lost all this time with you. Time I can't ever get back. Oh, Daddy, if I could go back, if I had a re-do button, then maybe things might have been different. Can you ever forgive me?"

When my tears finally subsided, I leaned in to give him a kiss. That's when I noticed that his eyes were gently fluttering and there was moisture around his eyes. *He could hear me.*

***

There were no lights on in the house when I pulled in. Although it was pitch black out, the house still looked pretty much unchanged. The front porch drooped a tad bit more than it used to. A wooden swing had replaced the two ancient wicker rocking chairs. There were some toys that were scattered across the yard, and there was a swing set between the house and Nana's house. The house appeared to have an energy, a sense of a carefree life, even though it never did for me.

Nana's cabin smelled of must, mildew and air freshener. Brandon and Charlotte had lived in the cabin their first few years of their marriage. When Charlotte was pregnant with her second child, they moved into the main house, and Mom and Dad moved into the cabin. Mom detested the cabin, which only added to her hostility. Thankfully, I was never around during that time.

The tiny cabin was just as I remembered. Roughly 700 square feet, it still had two bedrooms and a bathroom with a full-size tub and not much else. There were two recliners in front of the living room window with a panoramic view of the main house and farm. A small book shelf stood in the corner, with a radio sitting on top. There was no TV. The kitchen had a small oak table that would be round, except the two side flaps were down in order for it to fit. The table was shoved against the wall, with two small chairs. This cabin felt like…home.

My fondest memories of my childhood were of my Nana and me, sitting in her cabin, watching her crochet, or do puzzles, or cook. I would sit in there for hours and listen to her stories. She understood me more than my own Mom ever did. My Mother knew this, and she was not pleased.

Did Elvira pack half my closet? I thought as I trudged my enormous suitcase through the door. Panting, I grabbed my phone and sat down in the recliner. Still no response from Seth, I punched the off button, irate. There was no reason I shouldn't have heard from him by now. Rocking slowly, my body started to grow weary. As I relaxed, memories that I had kept at bay came flooding over me. Being here brought me right back to where it all started. I was right back to 1993, on Chokecherry Drive.

CHAPTER 3

JASON

"I'm not sure I understood you correctly. You don't want to come with us to Texas?" Mom asked, horrified.

"Really, Mom? You can't honestly expect me to follow you guys forever. I'm eighteen now." I really didn't want to start a fight, especially not on graduation night.

"Martin, aren't you going to say something?" Mom asked, looking for support.

Dad leaned back in his chair, his trademark toothpick traveling from one side of his mouth to the other. "Well," he finally said. "I reckon we can't keep him forever. Where do you plan on going, Son?"

I hesitated. "I'm not sure."

Mom sighed and pinched the bridge of her nose. "Jason, I don't expect you to follow us forever. However, the biggest part of being on your own is thinking things through. Do you want to stay around Fayetteville? You already have a job, so I am sure you can find a cheap place to rent."

I shook my head and Mom sighed again. Dad leaned in and patted her hand. "Loretta, give him a

21

chance to make up his mind. Ok, Son, lets figure this out. You don't want to stay here, and you don't want to come with us to Fort Hood. Any other ideas?"

"I was thinking…Minnesota," I said.

"Minnesota? As in, Grey Eagle, Minnesota? Jason, what on earth do you think is there for you?" Mom threw her hands up in the air.

I looked at Dad for help. He sat there, still moving that toothpick from side to side. Finally, he said, "Maybe you could stay with my parents for a while, until you figure out what it is you want."

I exhaled. He was on my side. Now, I just had to convince my mother.

"Do you know how hard it is going to be living with your grandparents? They live in the middle of nowhere, and you don't know anyone there."

"I don't know anyone here either, Mom. I have no friends, and I can find a job, milking cows, anywhere. There are plenty of farms around there. I can work a few years until I can save for a place of my own."

"You realize that you will need to help my parents out," Dad said. When I nodded, he continued. "I will call them after dinner and see what they say. You will need to step up and help them with all their yard work. You will get a job and pay rent. You will obey them and respect their house rules. Have I made myself clear?"

"Yes, sir," I answered.

"Okay, it's settled. After dinner I will call them and see what they say. Now let's enjoy the rest of our night together."

Mom sat there with her arms crossed, and her eyes closed, shaking her head.

***

Luckily, my belongings fit in two small boxes. Had I had more, it would not have all fit in my pickup truck. My Chevy was rusty, but I had faith that we would make it to Minnesota with little to no hiccups.

Mom fretted all morning. I appreciated it at first, but she was getting on my nerves. I needed to leave soon, just to put her out of her misery. She packed me a cooler with water, sandwiches, and chips so that I had to make less stops. I promised to call her every time I stopped for gas.

Dad came out of the house just as I loaded the cooler. "I just got off the phone with Grandpa. He said he lined up a job interview for you already."

"I could have done that on my own," I grumbled. Suddenly, I second guessed my decision. Was living with them going to be as bad as my overbearing Mother?

"I think he is pretty excited about you moving there, and he just wanted to help. When I talked to him last night, he said he knew of the perfect place. He called the farmer this morning and asked him if he needed any help. The guy said he was open to a job interview. So, when you get there and settled, all you need to do is give the guy a call and let him know when you can stop out."

Mom hugged me tighter. "Are you sure this is really what you want? You still have time to change your mind. You could still come with us."

I smiled. "Yes, Mom. I will be fine. If it doesn't work out, I will find my way back to Texas."

"Do you promise?" she asked.

"I promise."

Mom kissed my cheeks over and over and hugged me until I could barely breathe. I finally broke free and hopped in my truck. As I drove away, I saw them in the rear-view mirror. Dad's arms were wrapped around Mom, and she was waving goodbye with her handkerchief.

***

My rusty old blue pickup and I made it to Grey Eagle, Minnesota in thirty-one hours. I passed through one storm, four accidents, and a lot of construction. True to my word, I called Mom every time I stopped for gas. By the time I reached my grandparents, I was exhausted and knew my truck needed new brakes soon.

My grandparents were excited to see me, and I walked in, stomach growling, to find a feast waiting for me. Grandma made waffles, sausage, toast, fruit and orange juice.

"I figured you would be hungry," she said, giving me a hug. "And look how tired you are. You better eat and go lay down. Grandpa called Mr. Reilly and told him you would be by this afternoon for your interview. That should give you a few hours to sleep."

"Thanks Grandma. This smells delicious. I'm starving. But I better call Mom and let her know I am here, so she can finally settle down."

Grandma laughed. "I called her as soon as you pulled in. That girl sure loves you."

I nodded, not wanting to waste any time talking when I had all this food in front of me. It wouldn't take long to get used to this.

***

It was late afternoon by the time I unpacked, napped, and drove to Long Prairie to buy new brakes for my truck. Grandpa had a big garage with plenty of tools, so I could replace them tonight, after my job interview.

I slowed down when I spotted a black Ford

Tempo parked on the side of the road. As I drove around it, I noticed that the front left tire was flat. I spotted two girls up ahead, walking in the dreadful heat. Assuming it was their vehicle, I came to a complete stop when I approached them.

The job interview would just have to wait. What gentleman wouldn't help two pretty damsels in distress? Maybe Minnesota was just what I needed after all.

CHAPTER 4
MACY

"Who-hoo!" Leah shouted as the final bell rang. "Only one more year of this hell hole and we'll be free!"Despite the odd looks from everyone around us, I couldn't help but grin. She had a point.

It was unusually hot and humid, but that did not dampen our spirits as we went to my car. Some classmates were high-fiving each other, others were hugging and making promises to keep in touch over the summer. Living twenty minutes from Long Prairie, I made no such promises. I knew that my summer would be filled with farm work, and on the off chance that I did get some downtime, it would all be spent with Leah.

Leah Watson had been my best friend and neighbor since the third grade. Her parents owned the farm next door, which was only about a quarter mile away. We spent our summers biking up and down Chokecherry Drive, having sleep-over's at each other's houses, building forts, and playing tag on hay bales. As we got older, we spent a lot of time down by Willow's Pond, obsessing about cute boys and gossiping about the lame girls in our class.

Leah was my polar opposite. She was beautiful in a way I never would be. With her long, naturally wavy blonde hair, blue eyes, and clear skin, she turned heads all the time. My greasy freckle face was never short of at least one or two pimples. I often went unnoticed. I was known as the girl who was always with that hot chick. Leah was bold and fearless. I was a rule follower. She was outgoing, where I was shy. She wore name brand clothes, I did not. She was not expected to help on her family's farm, I had daily chores. Leah had better grades than me. I had to study twice as hard and twice as long as she did. She had more friends than me. Leah had everything I've ever wanted. Hell, she *was* everything I ever wanted. And even though I knew she was aware of our differences, somehow, she liked me anyway.

The one and only thing that I did have that she did not, was a car. My 1984 black Ford Tempo was nothing to brag about, with high miles and plenty of rust, but it did get me to and from school. This meant that it also got Leah to and from school. Leah was forever grateful that she did not have to ride the bus. It was not that her parents couldn't afford to get her a car. It was that her driving was terrible. Plus, Leah's parents always pitched in for gas, and we got to spend more time together.

The heat came rushing at us as we opened the car doors and hopped inside. My car didn't have air conditioning, so we cranked the windows down. Leah dug through my cassette tapes, popped in Janet Jackson, and turned the volume up. We sang our way out of town, fighting our hair back from the wind.

We were two miles to Grey Eagle on Highway 287 when my front left tire exploded. I grabbed the steering wheel with both hands and lifted my foot off the gas.

Leah quickly turned down the radio and held on tightly to her seat belt. The tire flopped around the rim, and my steering wheel started vibrating violently. We gradually slowed down, and I pulled over.

Leah squealed. "That was freaking awesome! You didn't freak out at all!"

I beg to differ, I thought as I looked around for my emergency flashers. Once they were activated, I got out to survey the damage.

"There's no fixing this," I muttered. "We're going to have to walk to town. We can call my Dad once we get there. He can come and get us."

The walk seemed to drag on and on. The sun reflected off the pavement making it feel even hotter than it was. My clothes felt damp against my skin, and my shorts were clinging to my legs, making them ride up in the middle. I kept pulling my shorts down as we walked, and I could feel sweat roll down into my bra. I glanced over at Leah as we walked. She showed no signs of discomfort or nasty sweat. She looked great actually.

"It's so hot out here," I gasped. I could not keep up with Leah's pace, not in this heat. And I probably could not keep up with her on any other given day either.

She slowed a little. "It sure is. Today would have been a perfect day to head down to Willow's Pond and test out the tire swing. Maybe we can if we get back in time?" Leah asked.

I nodded, it was too hard to walk and talk at the same time. Our pond was less than a quarter mile from our house in the empty cow pasture. There was a narrow foot path that led us to two big willow trees, which was why it was called "Willow's Pond." Leah and I would drag towels, small coolers, and floaties down there. Eventually, my father hung a tire swing on one of the trees and he made us a sitting bench with some old barn wood.

Leah and I spent three to four afternoons a week at the pond, much to my Mother's dismay. She couldn't see the pond from the front window, so she always sent my little brother Brandon check on us. We begged and pleaded for her to let us pitch a tent and spend the night out there, but she never agreed. She often stood in front of the living room window, her arms crossed, her lips pursed in a thin line, and murmuring under her breath when we would finally drag ourselves back home.

"You're going to waste half your life out there," she would say when I came in, shaking her head. "Obviously, I haven't given you enough to do around here." And on the days where my youth seemed to bother her the most, or when I was gone a little too long, my chore list seemed to get longer.

Glancing back at my car to gauge how far we'd come, I noticed there was a pickup heading our way. "Leah, someone's coming!" I shouted.

"Thank God," she said. "I didn't know how much farther I could walk out here."

A rusty blue Chevy pickup with a loud exhaust pulled up behind us. Leah and I both headed over to the driver's side window, hoping he would help us. His window was already rolled down when we approached.

"Need a ride?" the young man asked shyly. He had dirty blonde hair, piercing blue eyes, and a slightly crooked nose. He wasn't handsome, but he certainly was not ugly. He was somewhere in between. And he was definitely someone I had never seen around here before.

"Yes, we had a flat," I answered, my neck turning red from embarrassment.

"Do you have a spare? I can change it for you." The way his eyes lingered on mine made me blush. *What was wrong with me? Why was he looking at me like that?*

"I – I don't think so." I glanced away, hoping no one would notice. Apparently, I was wrong.

"You don't know if you have a spare?" Leah rolled her eyes, obviously extra animated in front of our rescuer.

"Hop in, I'll give you a lift," the driver said, starting his pickup back up.

Leah scurried off into the passenger side, clinching the middle seat. I hopped in after her and closed the heavy door, already dreading the ride before it began.

"Where to?" he asked.

"We live on Chokecherry Drive. Leah's on the Watson farm. I'm on the Reilly farm," I answered. He nodded, as if he knew exactly where that was.

"You don't look like you are from around here," Leah said as she leaned into him flirtatiously.

"Nope," our mystery man answered. After a pause, he added. "I'm Jason. Jason McNally."

Leah was just getting started. "Where do you live, Jason?" she asked, flipping her hair back.

"I just moved in with my grandparents. They live on Birch Lake." Jason didn't seem bothered by her questions, but he also didn't divulge any information.

"Oh, my," Leah pouted, batting her eye lashes, "What happened to your parents?"

"Oh nothing," he clarified. "They are in the military. They are moving again, and I decided I didn't want to go with. I just graduated, and I want to get a job and see what it's like to stay in one place for a while. Besides, my grandparents could use a little help around the house."

"Where did you live before coming here?" Leah asked.

"Fayetteville, North Carolina," Jason answered.

"What does your girlfriend think about you moving out here in the middle of nowhere?" Leah pressed. I inwardly groaned, she didn't realize how awful all her questions sounded. However, the mystery deepened with each question that Jason McNally responded to. For the first time since I got in his pickup, my eyes left the road to study Jason, waiting for his answer.

"No girlfriend." He must have sensed me staring because he glanced over at me, meeting my gaze. Our eyes held for the briefest moment, until I looked away. I felt my neck start to flush. Why should I care if this strange guy had a girlfriend or not?

"Are you getting a job around here?" Leah sounded hopeful.

"That's the plan," he said, turning into my driveway. Jason had to be relieved that Leah's interrogation was coming to an end.

Dad came walking from the barn, wiping his hands on an oil rag. Concern was written on his face when the three of us climbed out of the unfamiliar truck.

"What's wrong Macy?" he asked.

"I got a flat tire a few miles from town. Jason stopped to help us." I blurted. My neck and face reddened as all eyes were on me, including Jason's.

Dad looked over at Jason. "Thank you for bringing the girls home. I thought you were someone else. I thought you were here for a job interview."

"Oh, I am," Jason said, extending his hand. "I'm sorry I'm a little late. These two young ladies needed a ride. I'm Jason McNally."

CHAPTER 5
MACY

A soft knock on the door woke me from a fitful sleep. For a moment I was disoriented, waking with the sunlight beaming on my face. My stiff neck and tight back would be an annoying reminder that I slept in the rocking chair all night. With a mental note not to do that again, I went and answered the door.

"Good morning," Brandon said, although it seemed more like a question than a greeting. "Did you sleep well?"

"Not really," I stretched and yawned. "I fell asleep in the rocking chair and never made it to bed. Come on in."

"Oh, no, that's okay. I'll let you finish getting ready. I just wanted to let you know that Charlotte is making breakfast. The kids are excited to see you, too. Do you want to ride together to the nursing home?"

"Sure," I said. "I'll get ready and head on over."

Brandon stood there, as though there were something else he wanted to say. He must have decided against it, as he turned around and simply walked away.

I turned my phone back on and realized it was

already eight. Although it was only six at home, I tried calling Seth, and was surprised that he answered. He was obviously sleeping.

"Macy," he croaked out. "What's going on?"

"We have to meet with hospice in a few hours. Dad is not doing so well. It doesn't sound like it will be... much longer." Tears burned my eyes. I suddenly realized just how far away my world was from here, and right now all I wanted was my world back. I wanted to be home with Seth, Bree and Ella. The last thing I wanted to do was discuss my Father's final days, and the last place I wanted to be was in Grey Eagle. The memories cut much too deep.

"Oh babe, what can I do?" Seth was alert, and full of concern.

"I wish I knew. You are going to have to talk to the girls and let them know I might be here a few more days. What time did you get in last night?"

"I –ah, I ended up crashing here, in my office," Seth stammered. "There was no way I could drive. We celebrated a little too hard. I'm just about to head home and get the girls ready for school. But I am going to have to fly out to New York late this afternoon for Good Morning America. Will Elvira be able to stay with the girls?"

"She said she could, but how long are you going to be gone?" I asked. The only positive thing about being in the middle of nowhere was that I would not have to see all the tabloid covers with Asia Prescott's messy divorce splattered all over them, and all the public appearances that followed.

"Only a day, honey. We are taking Asia's private jet, so I will be back tomorrow afternoon. I can do the rest of the press around the girls' schedule. But if you need us to fly out there beforehand, I can always send someone else on my team for Asia's appearances."

"I'll keep you posted. Keep your phone with you. Give the girls a kiss for me as soon as you see them. Tell them I'll call them after school."

After hanging up, I still felt unsettled while I showered and dressed. Pinpointing exactly what was so unsettling was another matter. Something felt off. Was it being so far away from the girls? Or maybe it was because Seth had so much going on right then that he wasn't home with the kids?

Maybe it was because I had no idea how long I would be here. Would my Father live for hours, or days or weeks? Would I have to see him like he was last night, so lifeless and unresponsive, for days and days? The last thing I ever thought I would have to do was to watch him die.

Of course, it was all the above. To add to it, my relationship with Brandon was strained at best. The awkwardness was apparent and I hadn't even been here a full twenty-four hours. Charlotte and I were practically strangers. Brandon did not meet her until after I left for college. I had to think long and hard to remember all of their children's names, or when I even saw their kids last. If it wasn't for social media, I doubted I would even know what my nieces and nephews looked like. Regrettably, I had no one to blame but myself. I put the distance between us. I made the mistakes. And I worked so hard to never look back. Until now.

***

My heart was racing, and my hands were sweaty as I walked into Brandon and Charlotte's house, formerly my childhood home. It had been upgraded in my absence. They now had a dishwasher, updated appliances, updated paint colors and new vinyl flooring. Nevertheless, it still felt like this place belonged to my parents.

Charlotte was cooking eggs, hash-browns, bacon and sausage. Brandon was getting all the children settled at the table, until they realized I was there. The oldest one squealed, causing everyone to turn. The three kids hopped off their chairs and came running over, leaving the youngest child, Gideon, behind as he was buckled in his highchair. Brandon sat down, defeated.

"Auntie Macy!" Scarlet shouted as she threw her arms around my leg. The other two, Andrew and Stella, followed suit. "Come eat with us!"

"Ok, let's go sit down," I said, attempting to drag them back to their seats.

"They are a little excited," Charlotte explained, coming over for a hug. "It's good to see you, Macy. I hope you brought your appetite."

What I really needed was coffee, but I didn't spot a coffee maker. I merely nodded and sat down next to Andrew and Stella. Brandon sat at the head of the table, and Charlotte right next to him.

Charlotte asked how the girls were doing in school, and what activities kept them occupied. She asked about Seth and his job, and lastly, she asked about Asia Prescott. She wanted to know if I had ever met the movie star or her ex-husband, Augustus. Charlotte then wanted to know if we had ever been to any of Asia's homes, or if we have ever seen a live movie set. It was obvious that Charlotte was a huge fan.

My first and only encounter with Asia was by accident. The girls and I decided to surprise Seth and bring him lunch. Seth, two other lawyers, and Asia were all in his office when we arrived unannounced.

Seth met us at the door.

"What are you doing here?" he hissed.

"We thought we would bring you lunch," I said, peeking into the office. Seth's co-workers both looked away, pretending to not notice this uncomfortable exchange. Then I met Asia's cool gaze. She gave me the once over, with a look of total distain.

"This meeting just started, Hun. I'm afraid I can't have lunch right now." He knelt down and gave the girls a kiss and a hug. "You girls were so sweet to think of me and bring me lunch. What a wonderful surprise. But I'm in a meeting right now, so I can't step out. But I'll be home in time for dinner." He closed the door in our faces. We were dismissed.

That was the last time we would ever surprise him for lunch. It was also the last time I wore khaki capri's, a white t-shirt, a gray zip-up long sleeve shirt and flip-flop sandals to his office. Never again would I show up looking as frumpy as I did that day.

But I told Charlotte none of this, nor did I tell her that that night ended in a two-and-a- half hour fight. Instead, I told her that I met Asia once at Seth's office, but I wasn't able to stick around to get to know her. That seemed to pacify Charlotte, or at least she didn't press further as it was time for us to leave. Charlotte shooed me away when I offered to help clean up.

"I got this. You go spend some time with your Dad," she said. This was the longest amount of time I had ever spent with Charlotte, and I enjoyed it. Maybe we could get to know each other after all.

***

Thankfully Brandon needed gas, so we were able to stop in town for coffee. Grey Eagle appeared to be the same on the surface. Main Street still had two gas stations, a bar, post office, grocery store, library and a laundromat. The elementary school was now closed, but the building was still standing solid. Grey Eagle was a place I despised for years, but, driving down Main Street made me realize how unfair that was. I had to admit, it wasn't the town I hated so much, it was the actual events that had happened here. Would the pain and remorse ever fully go away?

Brandon broke the ice first. "Is there anything you need from Long Prairie while we are there?" he asked.

"Not that I can think of," I answered. "I just can't believe Dad went downhill so fast. He sounded just fine when I spoke with him on the phone, and that was just a few weeks ago. And now, here we are, discussing his final days."

"He's been going downhill for a while, Macy. Dad hasn't been himself for months. He hasn't been eating much and he's sleeping all the time. Hell, he didn't even know who the kids were when I brought them last. He thinks Mom is still alive and he can't figure out why she hasn't been coming to see him."

"I didn't know any of this," I said. "I guess no one thought to tell me."

"Yeah, well, you weren't here." Brandon grumbled.

The accusation took me by surprise, although it shouldn't have. Seth and I gladly took on the financial burden of my father's care. It was the least we could do. And I knew I wasn't here to see the daily decline like Brandon was. If there was one thing I learned from years of therapy, was that we could not go back in time and change a single thing, no matter how much we wanted to. But now was not the time to pick a fight, so I chose my next words carefully.

"You're absolutely right, Brandon. I'm sorry I wasn't around more. I wish things could have been different. I wish I could go back and change, well, everything."

"Aw, hell, I didn't mean to start anything, Macy. I understand why you left. But this hasn't been easy for me. I'm running the farm, taking care of Dad, then there's Charlotte and the kids. Some days it feels like there ain't enough of me to go around."

I nodded, knowing all too well how Brandon was feeling. No comforting words or advice would change how he felt. He had a lot on his plate, and it was easy to see that. Maybe I wasn't being totally fair in my judgment of Brandon and his happy-go-lucky life. There was nothing plain or simple about his life.

"So...are you going to see him while you are here?" Brandon asked, changing the subject.

"See who?"

"You know who I am talking about, Macy."

I shrugged. "Does he even live around here anymore?"

"He never left." He answered, pulling into the Long Prairie Nursing Home. "Now, let's get this shit show over with."

***

It was almost dinnertime by the time we got back to Brandon and Charlotte's. We met with Sandy, Gracie and the hospice team first. They talked about how my father's skin color was changing; his hands and feet were now a bluish-purple color. He hadn't eaten or drank anything in several days and was no longer having bowel movements. He was rarely awake, and on the off chance that he was, he was disoriented and had no idea who any of us were. Both Sandy and Hospice agreed; my father would not live but another two or three days.

There wasn't much we needed to do about his final arrangements. His funeral was set up for him when Mom died five years ago. Sandy graciously called the funeral home to start the process, while Brandon and I spent time with Dad. Gracie came in to check on Dad twice during our visit, checking his pulse, the monitors and making sure we had a glass of water or coffee. Her cheerful voice and kind smile was welcoming, and it was easy to see how much she cared about him.

Our visit was quiet, seeing as how I said most of what I needed to say to my Father the night before. Brandon and I sat across from each other, each holding my Father's cold hand, lost in our own thoughts. Brandon stayed for almost an hour, and then he left to run a few errands. While I was grateful for the time alone, the lump in my throat stopped me from being able to say anything out loud to him.

Realizing we skipped lunch, we picked up several pizzas on our way back to the farm. Charlotte was relieved to have the night off from cooking, and the kids were thrilled that I was spending another night in Nana's cabin. Scarlet comprehended most of what was going on, and she kept repeating to her younger sister and brothers, "Auntie Macy is here because Grandpa is going to Heaven." Luckily, that didn't faze them.

We ate supper on the front porch and shared a few glasses of wine while the kids played on the swing set. Despite the circumstances, it was a beautiful evening. The mosquitoes hadn't peaked yet, and suddenly I knew what I had to do.

"Do either of you ever go down to Willow's Pond?" I asked.

"Oh no," Brandon said. "I haven't been down there in years. We moved the cows out to that pasture last fall because the grass was starting to get too long."

"The kids are too young to go down there," Charlotte added. "We keep a little pool up here in the summer, until they get older."

"I think I'm going to take a walk down there," I said, finishing off my wine. "And then, I better just call it a night."

"Watch out for the cow pies," Brandon said, smiling.

"If I find one, I'll bring it back for you," I grinned. We'd never been able to banter back and forth like this before. A silver lining, perhaps?

Before I headed out to the pond, I called Seth and filled him in. I spoke with Elvira, who assured me that she was fine staying there as long as I needed, and that she had everything under control. The girls were doing great and hadn't missed a homework assignment, extra-curricular activity, or home-cooked meal. Lastly, I spoke with Bree and Ella. They had so many questions and concerns regarding their Grandpa, and they were missing me terribly. I comforted them as best I could over the phone, but even I knew it was pointless.

I tried changing the subject. "What are you going to do tomorrow?"

"Swim! And guess who's coming over to swim with us?" Ella asked.

"Is it your friend Amy, from school?" I guessed.

"No, it's Daddy's friend, Asia! She is going to come over and swim with us!" Ella exclaimed.

"Oh, she is," I replied, a little more curtly than I intended. "That's great sweetheart. Can I talk to your Dad again?"

Seth cleared his throat and got back on the line. "Hey, babe."

"Is there something you need to tell me?" I asked

through clenched teeth.

"Now Macy, this isn't a big deal. She knew the girls were missing you and she just wants to come and hang out with them, to help get their minds off things. What was I supposed to do, tell her no? She is my highest paying client."

"Why didn't you mention this before?"

"Because I was worried about you and I forgot all about it. She is just coming to play with the girls. If you want me to cancel, I will. The girls aren't used to not having you around and I thought they would have a lot of fun with her. It will take their minds off Howard." He sounded apologetic. "You have nothing to worry about."

I sighed. "You're probably right. I'm sure they would have fun. I'm sorry. This is all so overwhelming. I don't like being this far away from home."

"Babe, I've got this. We are all fine over here. We will fly out there, as soon as you are ready for us. We miss you, too."

"I love you," I said.

"Love you, too, Macy. Call me tomorrow."

Feeling uneasy, I grabbed my favorite sweatshirt, changed into sneakers and headed out to Willow's Pond before I changed my mind. Why would a movie star like Asia Prescott want to hang out with my girls and my husband? Was it a coincidence that she was coming to my home, while I was thousands of miles away? Why didn't Seth mention this before? Was I reading too much into it?

I contemplated this while heading down the narrow path to the pond. The path was smaller than I remembered, and Brandon was right about how overgrown the pasture had become. There were about twenty beef cattle huddled together on the east end of the pasture. There were no fresh cow pies for me to return to Brandon. I was far enough away to not bother them, but close enough so that they could watch every move I made.

The willow trees were smaller than I remembered. The tire swing was still tied to the tree, but the rope was frayed and needed to be replaced. The bench that my father made for us out of old barn wood was still there, tarnished from years of Minnesota's harsh winters.

Taking a deep breath, I sat down on that rickety bench, and looked out at the pond. This spot held all my greatest memories, and unfortunately some painful ones too. Willow's Pond knew all the dirty, dark secrets of my past. And now that I was here, I knew I needed to let out everything I had been holding back. I could no longer ignore what happened, even though it was too late to change any of it. It was time to face the biggest mistake of my life, I decided, as unwelcomed tears began to fall.

CHAPTER 6
MACY

MAY 1993
GREY EAGLE, MINNESOTA

"Oh my God, Macy! I can't believe Jason is getting a job on your farm. He is so hot!" Leah was practically drooling.

"Shhh," I said, grabbing her arm and pulling her away from Jason's truck. "Do you have to shout? I'm sure he heard that."

"I hope he did," she said as she turned back to check. I couldn't help but glance back too, but since Dad was leading him over to the barn, I doubted he heard Leah's embarrassing remarks. My Father never mentioned that he was interviewing anyone, much less interviewing someone like Jason. Brandon and I usually helped with chores and planting now that school was out.

"Do you want to head over to Willow's Pond?" I suggested, trying to divert Leah's attention.

"Hell no," Leah said, sitting down on the front porch. "I need to see how this all plays out. If he gets a job here, I will be over here all summer. I can't believe he's going to work here."

"I'll grab some lemonades," I sighed, leaving Leah

to her daydreaming. I wished this whole job interview exchange wouldn't have happened in front of Leah. Leah was serious. If Jason did get this job, Leah would be over now, more than ever. Normally, that would be fine under any other circumstance, but I knew I would be watching Leah throw herself at him all summer, until they started dating. Then I'd be nothing more than a third wheel, and the farm would be the stepping stone to their relationship.

It wasn't that I liked him. No, that wasn't it at all. Jason McNally wasn't even that good looking. I mean, maybe he came off a little mysterious. Well, actually, quite intriguing. His slight southern accent proved that he had been places. He had seen more of the world than I ever will. Why he would settle to live on Birch Lake and work on the farm was something I may never know. But no, there was no way I would be ever be interested in dating someone like Jason. I just didn't want Leah to date him, that's all.

Mom pulled into the yard at the same time I stepped out with the lemonades.

"How was the last day of school, girls?" Mom asked.

"Fine," Leah and I answered in unison.

"Why are you both sitting out here in this dreadful heat?" she asked, dabbing her forehead with a tissue.

"We just want to catch another glimpse of your newest employee," Leah said.

"Employee? Oh, that's right, I almost forgot. Mr. and Mrs. McNally's grandson just moved in. Mr. McNally called a few days ago asking if there was anything we needed help with out here. Not sure why this young fellow couldn't find a job on his own. And you know your Father. He doesn't have the heart to say no." She shook her head.

"Macy, where is your car?" she asked, noticing it was missing for the first time.

"We got a flat tire on our way home from school, right outside of Grey Eagle. We started walking, but then this Jason stopped and gave us a ride home," I explained, hoping my face was not turning red at the mere mention of his name. Neither my Mother nor Leah seemed to notice.

"Here they come now!" Leah said, sucking in her breath.

All three of us watched intently as Dad led Jason out of the barn and toward the house. Jason was getting a tour of the place, pausing and nodding along as Dad would point out things now and then. He showed Jason the barn, pole shed, garage, Nana's cabin and pointed out the pastures and fields around the house.

"Elaine, this is Mr. and Mrs. McNally's grandson, Jason. He is going to be working here this summer," Dad said as they approached the house. "Jason, this is Mrs. Reilly."

"Nice to meet you, Mrs. Reilly," Jason said, with a slight nod. He was too far away to offer a hand shake, as Leah and I were sitting on the front porch steps, blocking him. My Mother stood behind us, sizing him up. Her disapproval was written all over her face as she checked him out from head to toe, lingering on the holes in his jeans and his worn-out boots.

"You as well," she answered coolly. Hearing the phone ring from the house, she turned and went inside.

"Well, Macy," Dad said. "Jason offered to replace your tire on his way home, so I can finish chores before supper. There's a spare in the garage. Jason, thank you again for helping Macy today, I appreciate it. We'll see you tomorrow morning."

"Thank you, sir," Jason said, shaking his hand. He

turned and looked at me, and for a moment I was sure he knew that his blue eyes were tearing deep into my soul. "You ready?"

"I sure am!" Leah interjected as she jumped off the porch. "I'll sit in the middle!"

"Not so fast," Mom yelled as she stepped out onto the porch. "Leah, your Mother called. She needs you to head on home now. You are having company for supper."

Leah stopped abruptly and turned around. She gave Jason the best smile she could muster, disappointment written all over her face. For a brief second, her eyes narrowed when she looked directly at me, and then gave Jason one last smile. "I guess I'll see you guys tomorrow." With a slight wave, she started home.

Watching Leah walk away, with her shoulders sagging slightly, I knew that look was a warning sign. I'd seen her give this look to others, when other people had gotten in her way. The outcome was never pretty. But this was the first time she had ever glared at me like that. The message rang loud and clear. I was to stay away from Jason McNally. Leah had officially claimed him as hers.

But Leah had no reason to be jealous of me. It was inconceivable to think that our friendship hung on the balance of someone she had just met. It was not my fault that he happened to pick us up on the side of the road today. And it wasn't my fault that my Father hired him either. So, what was she so worried about? There was no way anyone, including Jason, would ever be attracted to someone like me.

The start of my summer was beginning to look a little glum. Clearly my Mother was not impressed with the new hired hand. My best friend's interests took a sudden turn when she set her eyes on Jason. Leah wouldn't be over to hang out with me anymore. She would only be here to see Jason, and she was determined to make him notice her. They would be dating in no time, and I had no desire to be anyone's third wheel. Maybe hiring this guy wasn't such a good idea after all.

***

The heat hadn't subsided by the next morning. My shorts and tank top were already sticking to me by the time I headed to the milk parlor. Brandon's job was to feed and water the beef cows, calves, chickens, and dogs. Dad was already in the fields planting, which left me to show Jason how to use our milking machine. I'd never had to show anyone how to milk cows before, much less someone I barely even knew.

But after the awkward ride back to my car the previous night, I was surprised he even showed up. Neither of us spoke the entire truck ride. He seemed content to hang out in silence, and he didn't appear to be uncomfortable at all. I sat as far away from him as possible, leaning hard against the passenger door, staring out the window. I was careful not to look in his direction. It was too hot to stay in his truck while he changed my tire, so I stood off to the side, and only glanced his way when I was certain he couldn't see me looking at him. I think I muttered a "thank you" as I hopped in my car, but I was not even sure he heard me. When I peeked through my rear-view mirror, he was grinning. Who knows what he found so amusing, but I felt like a total fool. He followed me all the way back into town, until I had to take a left turn, where he had to take a right.

Much to my dismay, Jason leaned against the

parlor door, waiting for me with the same grin on his face from the evening before. He was wearing another pair of jeans with holes in them, the same worn out boots, a cut off t-shirt and baseball cap.

"Good morning," he said. "It looks like it's going to be another scorcher today."

"Have you been waiting long?" I asked, wanting to cut the small talk short. I could feel my neck start to turn red, and it had nothing to do with the heat.

"No, I just got here a few minutes ago."

"Oh good," I said. "Let's get this over with." Jason stepped aside, letting me lead the way.

Luckily, Jason was a quick learner, and rarely asked questions. He listened intently while I showed him the parlor, the milk tanks, and where to find the supplies. After we put on latex gloves, I showed him where the iodine solution was. I explained to him how to dip it on all the teats without getting the udders wet. Using separate paper towels, we carefully dried off the teats thoroughly. Then I taught Jason how to apply the teat cups correctly and how each cow milks for roughly five to seven minutes. After detaching the machine at the end of the milking, we once again cleaned the teats with iodine solution, and dried them, to help avoid mastitis. The cows then go into the next room of the parlor, where they eat and drink. This stops them from sitting down in their own manure and decreases the risk for infection.

The whole process took several hours, with only twelve cows being milked at a time. Chokecherry farm was milking roughly two hundred cows, and we were milking twice per day. After all the milking was done, the parlor needed to be hosed down to wash out any manure. It was a dirty job, but Jason didn't seem to care.

Even though we were in such close proximity, I tried to stay as far away from him as possible. He was so close I could smell his cologne. The mixture was both musky and clean. When our arms brushed together as we both reached for the paper towels, I quickly backed up. Jason smiled, and then handed me the paper towel before grabbing one for himself.

Why was this guy having such an effect on me? I could not stand near him without turning beet red. There were not any boys in my class that caused me to have this sort of reaction. They were all so immature and self-centered. But every time I even looked at Jason, I got so flustered that I didn't know how to act. I had never been more self- conscious. He knew the effect he was having on me, too. I was certain of it.

"Good morning," Leah practically sang as she walked into the parlor. "Oh Jason, you're in here too. How's it going?"

Leah was wearing a black and white polka dot bikini top with low cut denim shorts. The front button was undone, showing her matching bikini bottoms underneath.

"Good," Jason said, not looking up from where he was spraying.

"Ugh, it stinks in here," Leah said. "Macy, are you almost done? Let's head down to the pond. I need to work on my tan."

"Sounds good to me. We're just finishing up," I said. "How was your dinner last night?"

Leah rolled her eyes. "It was so stupid. I don't even know why I needed to be there. It was just my aunt and uncle over and they left right after dinner."

Leah waited until we were finished, and the three of us walked out together. She followed close behind Jason, trying hard to get his attention.

"Jason, would you like to come down to the pond with us? It sure is hot out here," Leah said, making an extra effort to fan herself.

"No, thanks," Jason said. "I'll go see if Brandon needs any help until Mr. Reilly gets back."

Leah was persistent. "Well, stop down when you are done. Don't let this day go to waste."

"Will you need help with milking later?" I asked Jason, looking directly into his eyes.

"I think I can manage," he winked.

So, this was what having butterflies felt like.

***

Leah and I spent the afternoon alternating between floating on floaties in the pond and lying under the shade trees. It was humid and sticky, but the water was still too cold to stay in it for long. My skin felt hot to the touch, even after applying sunscreen several times.

Leah desperately wanted to know what happened on the ride back to my car the night before. She wanted to know everything Jason said, everything we talked about, and how long we were together. Although she didn't seem too disappointed that neither of us had much to say, she was still hoping to learn anything she could about him. She carried on about him all afternoon, even as we walked back up to the house early that evening.

Mother and Nana were sitting on the front porch, bibles in hand, when we approached. "I see you did not do any of your household chores, Macy," she said, closing the book. "One day into summer break and I came home to a mess."

"I-I'm sorry," I stammered, looking down at my feet. "I forgot all about it."

"Oh, that was my fault, Mrs. Reilly. I was so

excited to get back down to the pond in this heat. I guess I came earlier than I should have." Leah said.

Mother looked at both of us, unconvinced. "Well," she said after a moment. "I guess the chores you missed today will get added to your list for tomorrow. Now, Nana needs to run some errands in Long Prairie. Since no one thought to start supper, I guess I will need to do that. So, Macy, go get some clothes on and take Nana to the store."

"Okay," I replied, "but what about milking? Do I need to stay and help Jason?"

"I don't see why you would need to. He worked at a farm at his previous job and has milked cows for years. At least that's what his grandfather told Dad."

I raced to my room to change clothes. So that's why Jason had no questions this morning. He let me ramble on and on, explaining how the whole entire process of milking cows worked. And the entire time, he already knew. How did I not notice this earlier? But the question that nagged me the most was, why didn't he say anything?

As Nana and I pulled out of the driveway, I turned to wave at Leah. I assumed she was heading home. But when I saw her, she was touching Jason's arm, her head tilted back, laughing at whatever it was he was saying.

CHAPTER 7
MACY

Much to my Mother's dismay, my Father really enjoyed having Jason around. My Dad found tasks and all sorts of repairs for Jason to do—things that Dad had long ago put off and never got around to fixing. Not only did Jason have skills in milking cows—which he failed to share with me— but he was also handy when it came to repairing equipment and changing the oil. He helped cut firewood and fixed fence posts. Many of our fence posts were rotten, some even knocked down, and dozens needed to be replaced. He helped mow the lawn and even tilled my Mother's garden.

He did all of this without complaint. He was quiet and unassuming when he worked, and he was quick to offer to pitch in or to start a new project without being told. More than once I saw my Dad nod in approval, obviously impressed with his work, although my Father was never one to offer any praise. Jason even found time to help Brandon with his chores. He carried pails of water to the chickens and helped clean out the chicken pens. Brandon took to him immediately, and he talked about him non-stop.

Two weeks on the job, and Mom still had not changed her opinion of him, and she had no plans to do so. According to her, he was not worthy enough to work on our farm. Jason showed up every day in worn out old boots, and tons of rips and stains in his jeans and t-shirts. Mother made snide remarks often, until Dad finally told her to stop one night at dinner. After that, she remained tight-lipped around my Father, but made sure that both Brandon and I knew what she thought of the guy who couldn't even wear a decent shirt to work. "He won't be here long," she warned. "Not a boy like that. There is no way he is going to stick around and take care of his elderly grandparents. He's nothing more than a drifter. Mark my words, he'll go back to where he came from in no time."

Even Nana seemed to like him. She would make him ham sandwiches and fresh chocolate chip cookies and bring him ice-cold water each day at noon, even though he came with a packed cooler every day. Jason had fixed a leak on the roof of her cabin, and he helped her move a part of a peony plant that was getting too big. Ever since then, she found things around her cabin that she needed him to look at. Nana was lonely, and he was kind to her.

Leah, too, never missed a chance to see Jason. She held off every day until close to noon, when I had finished morning milking and most of my chores list. If my chores weren't done by the time she got there, she used that as an opportunity to flirt with him. Although we were only heading to the pond each day, she still showed up with her makeup and hair done. I had to admit, she was trying really hard and she looked damn good. "I think he likes me," she'd say each day at the pond. She was extremely confident that he would be asking her out soon.

Although I was not a morning person, I somehow jumped out of bed to get ready for morning milking. It was an opportunity to see Jason, and the only time we got to be alone together. My shyness was slowly fading, and I didn't turn beet red every time I saw him anymore. I found myself stealing glances his way when I thought he wasn't looking, and, more often than not, he caught me, and would smile in return. There was no way I would get away with putting on makeup, doing my hair, and doing morning chores in a bikini. And I would never look as sexy as Leah. I knew I looked frumpy, with my hair back in a pony tail and tucked in a baseball cap. He saw me every day in a tank top and shorts, and my rubber boots with manure caked on them.

The more time I spent with him, the more I liked him. I've never had a crush like this on anyone. However, I was painfully aware that it would be no more than a crush, and a secret one at that. For one, there was no way someone like Jason would ever be interested in someone like me. And second, my best friend was head over heels in love with him, and she was doing whatever she could to be with him. If she ever had an inkling of my feelings, she would have been livid and our friendship would have been destroyed. It was already clear that she was jealous that he worked on my farm, and not hers. She tried to get her parents to hire Jason, but they knew how much help he was to my Dad, and they did not pursue him any further.

It was agonizing listening to Leah carry on and on about how handsome he was, their flirtations, and how he was getting really close to asking her out. Leah gushed about every look they shared, every conversation they'd ever had, and she analyzed each word he said. All the while, I kept silent. After all, I could never share my secret. Instead I did what any best friend would do. I encouraged her. Eventually they would be together anyway, and I would be happy for both of them. I really had no other choice, no matter how much it stung.

"Oh, for heaven's sakes," I snapped one afternoon. "Just ask him out already!"

"Well, you would think he would have asked me out by now. What's taking him so long? Does he ever say anything about me?" Leah asked.

"No, he never talks about you," I answered, a little more shortly than I intended.

Leah pouted. "Fine, I will ask him out. I'll do it today, on our way back."

Ugh, why did I have to open my big mouth? Clearly, she had made up her mind. There was no way Jason would turn down someone as beautiful as Leah. I was certain of it. If I had just kept my mouth shut, maybe this wouldn't have happened so fast.

My stomach was in knots as we hauled our floaties and wet towels back up to the house later that afternoon. Dad and Jason were cutting wood and stacking it on the wood pile. Leah and I spotted him immediately. He saw us and nodded, all the while, he kept the same pace as my Dad.

"Ugh, your Dad is with him," Leah pouted. "I wonder if I should wait this out or just ask him out tomorrow."

"Well, it's not like he's going to say no," I blurted, instantly regretting my words. Silently I chided myself. If I didn't get my act together, both Jason and Leah would know soon enough of my ridiculous crush. I quickly changed my attitude. "Why don't we just wait on the front porch? It looks like they are almost done."

They were finishing stacking wood about the same

time Mom came home from work. Mother got out of the car, and looked from us on the front porch, over to Dad and Jason, then back at us again. Her lips pursed into a thin line, and she shook her head while she grabbed her purse and lunch bag out of the car. Unfortunately, she was never one to hold back what she was thinking.

"Have you girls been sitting out here all day, staring at the hired help?" she asked, irritated. "I'm sure there were better things you could be doing with your time."

Leah was quick to write off my Mother's accusations. She laughed. "Oh, Mrs. Reilly, we just got back from Willow's Pond. We thought we would dry off before I went home."

"I'm no fool. That boy is trouble, Leah. I would steer clear, if I were you," my Mother insisted. "That boy is pure trash."

Leah never answered her, but she stood up and started grabbing her belongings. Dad was heading to the house, which meant it was Leah's only chance to catch Jason before he left for the day. Leah looked back at me, and I whispered "good luck" to her. She smiled back, knowing I meant it. And I did mean it. I really was rooting for her.

I ran upstairs to my room to change out of my swimsuit before I went to help prepare dinner and set the table. But my nosiness got the best of me, so I peeked out my bedroom window, to see if I could see anything.

Jason was leaning up against the tailgate of his pickup, facing the house. Leah had her back to me, twirling her hair with the one hand and holding her wet towel with the other. They were deep in conversation, but it was hard to tell how it was going from how far away I was.

The conversation started to look uncomfortable. I couldn't read his expression, but he almost looked – mad? Annoyed? Without realizing it, I inched closer to the window. All of a sudden, Jason looked up at my window, making direct eye contact with me. I jumped back, mortified that I was intruding on their private moment. My heart started pounding, and my face flushed. I stood back, not sure what I should do next. Did I dare peek at them again? No, once was enough. I sat on my bed, taking deep breaths, and wiping my sweaty hands on my bedspread.

When I heard his truck rev up, I rushed to the window again, this time not caring who saw me. Jason was driving away, and Leah was walking home, her shoulders slumped in defeat. What the hell happened out there?

Before Mom wondered what was taking me so long, I ran downstairs and jumped right into dinner preparations. Dad was grilling steaks, so I fried potatoes and carrots, sliced homemade bread, and cut up strawberries and set out cream cheese dip. I set the table and got pitchers of lemonade and water. Brandon summoned Nana when dinner was ready.

Even with listening to Mom ramble on about who stopped in the bank today, I couldn't get my mind off Jason and Leah. What did she say to him that made him look so pissed? Why did he look up at me? Was he mad that I was watching? I tried to tune into the conversation at the dinner table. Nana wasted no time in bringing up her new favorite person.

"I made some chocolate chip cookies for Jason, so I brought over some extra ones before they go bad," Nana said. "I knew the kids would like them."

"I don't know why you bother," Mom said, rolling

her eyes. "I'm not sure why everyone around here isn't seeing what I'm seeing, but you all will one day."

"Elaine," Dad warned, trying to put a stop to her ranting. "He's an extremely hard worker, and I am glad to have him here. We are getting caught up on things that we haven't looked at in years."

"Yeah, and he helps me with all of my chores," Brandon said defensively. "He's really nice to me."

"I can see the effect he has on everyone, especially Leah. I have never seen a girl so desperate. Walking around here half naked and her face caked with all that make-up. Maybe I should call her Mother and let her know how she's behaving around that boy."

I knew better than to chime into this conversation. Whether I agreed or disagreed, she would take it upon herself to call Mrs. Watson if she thought I had an opinion on it. Hell, she might do it anyway, if she gave it anymore thought. But the message was crystal clear. None of us were to get too close to Jason McNally. She couldn't control my Father, but she sure as hell could control the rest of us.

CHAPTER 8

JASON

No matter how hard I tried, I couldn't get that girl out of my mind. I don't know exactly what it was that drew me to her, but, somehow, she invaded my thoughts when I was least expecting it. The more I was around her, the more I actually thought about being *with* her. She was beautiful and she didn't even know it.

There was a reason fate brought me to her rescue that day, and I could have hollered when I realized she lived on the Reilly farm. Maybe I should have told her that I already knew how to milk cows, but I just wanted to hear her soft voice. I could have listened to her for hours.

She turned red when she looked at me. She tried to look away, but her beautiful eyes ended up finding me anyways. That's because I couldn't keep my eyes off her. This job was the best job I've ever had. Spending time with Macy was the highlight of my day, even though it was such a short time.

Then her obnoxious friend showed up and ruined everything. Macy's eyes went dark, and she shied away, not willing to look at me the way she did when no one else was around. Leah was attractive and she knew it. The way she flaunted herself in her bikinis and all that make-up she wears was a complete turnoff. She was desperate. She tried too hard and frankly, she was annoying as hell.

So, imagine my surprise when Leah walked up out of the blue and told me I should take her on a date. I should have known it was coming, but I was caught off guard. She waited for me near my pickup, her hair and swimsuit still damp.

"Ask me," she said, twirling her hair.

"Ask you what?" I asked cluelessly.

She rolled her eyes and smirked. "Jason, you know what I am talking about. Ask me on a date."

It took me a second to realize that she was serious. I cleared my throat. "Um, I'm sorry, Leah. I couldn't ask you on a date."

"Well...why not? Don't you like me?"

"Leah, I think you are great...as a friend," I said, hoping she would let this go.

She frowned. "This makes no sense. Why don't you want to go out with me?"

I glanced up and saw Macy watching us from her upstairs window.

"Because, Leah, my heart belongs to someone else."

"Who?" she asked.

"I'm sorry, Leah. I gotta get going. My grandparents are waiting for me." Without waiting for her to respond, I hopped in my truck.

Had I been reading the signs all wrong? I thought Macy liked me as much as I liked her. Why on earth would she want me to date someone like Leah? Maybe she hadn't been flirting with me these past few weeks.

Maybe she didn't like me at all. Man, I really missed the mark on this one.

CHAPTER 9
MACY

Heavy wind and rain raged through the night, including marble sized hail. I was unable to sleep, but my mind was not on the storm as the night passed. I wished I would have stayed outside earlier, at a distance, so I could have talked to Leah before she left. As I tossed and turned, I realized that there could only be two reasons why Jason would turn someone as beautiful as Leah down. One reason could be that he already had a girlfriend, which didn't seem that far-fetched. I had no way of knowing what he did or who he hung out with after he left for the day. Or two, maybe my Mother was right after all. Maybe Jason was planning on high-tailing it out of here as soon as he could. Maybe he was an actual flight risk. Somehow, that idea seemed unimaginable.

The storm knocked down several tree branches. One of them had fallen on the corner of the pole shed, causing the corner of the roof to cave in. Thankfully that was the extent of the damage, but most of the day was spent on clean up.

The unbearable heat and humidity was gone the next morning as I headed out to the parlor. Brandon worked on clearing out the brush in and around the garden. My father surveyed the pole shed and started the clean up inside. Nana walked around her cabin, checking out her broken flower pots and damaged bushes.

Jason had already started milking by the time I got there. He didn't greet me when I came in. I sensed that he was doing his best to pretend I wasn't there. We worked in uncomfortable silence. He was dodging me, and I could only take the awkward silence for so long.

"What's got you in such a mood this morning?" I asked, hoping to lighten things up.

"Nothing," he said, focusing on the cows.

I shrugged. "Suit yourself." He was definitely brooding. It probably had to do with something Leah said. She must have offended him in some way. The next two hours felt like an eternity. He was not his usual self, joking and laughing, and we were certainly not working together as a team.

We were just finishing up when Jason turned and looked at me. "Why do you want me to date your friend?" He looked...hurt.

"Well...she likes you," I stammered.

"Do you think I should go out with her?" he asked, taking a step closer to me.

Instinctively, I took a step back, leaning up against the door. "Why are you asking me?"

He inched closer and looked right into my eyes. "Are you really that oblivious, Macy?" he whispered.

"I...I don't know what you're talking about," I stammered, staring back at him.

"Well, if I go out with her," he whispered again, "then I can't go out with you." He leaned in and kissed me softly on the lips. Jason stepped back, gauging my reaction. Before I could think about what was happening, I cupped the back of his head with my hands and pulled him to me, kissing him hard.

"Wait, wait, wait," I pulled away, trying to clear my head. "Are you sure you like me?"

Jason laughed. "I've thought about you day and night ever since I picked you up on the side of the road. You tried so hard not to look at me. Except when Leah asked if I had a girlfriend." I blushed hotly at the memory.

Jason leaned in and kissed me again, this time more passionately. We were both breathless when we finally got control of ourselves. Milking should have been done a while ago, and if we were gone much longer Brandon, or worse yet, my father, would come searching for us.

With one last kiss, we both walked out together. Brandon was making headway raking, and Dad was waiting for Jason, so they could remove the tree branch that was still sitting on the pole shed. I started piling up the larger sticks, never taking my eyes off Jason. I watched as he climbed up the shed with a chainsaw, cutting down the branch in several large pieces.

I have never experienced butterflies before Jason. I couldn't stop smiling. Although I had entertained the idea of being with him, I always told myself it would never be anything more than a fantasy. But he liked me back. We stole glances at each other the rest of the day. Jason watched me as much as I watched him, and he would wink at me each time he caught me staring. I could get lost gazing into his gorgeous eyes. I couldn't stop thinking about those wonderful kisses, and how much I wanted to do it again.

Nana made us ham sandwiches and cookies for

lunch, as we were all still working diligently in the yard. It was looking pretty good by then, and the four of us sat down on the porch to eat. Jason and I played it cool, and I was certain that Dad didn't suspect a thing. Jason was sitting on the porch swing when I handed him a glass of ice water, and when his hand brushed against mine, I instantly got goose bumps. Startled, I looked up, and saw him watching me curiously. He smiled, and I realized he was feeling the exact same way.

It was half past one when we all got back to work to finish cleaning up the storm's mess. Suddenly it dawned on me. Leah never showed up today. *Oh God. Leah.*

CHAPTER 10

MACY

Leah didn't show up the next day, or the day after that. It was four days later before she ventured back. She was a little standoffish at first, as though she wasn't quite sure how to behave now that she knew Jason did not have the same feelings. Leah still wore her sexiest bikini, and her hair was still pristine. She did relax a little on the makeup, which made her look more beautiful than before. It made no sense to me why Jason was attracted to someone as plain as me, and not someone like her. She had all the attributes that made men's heads turn, yet Jason had no interest in her whatsoever.

I was putting the mop away in the entryway closet when I saw Leah walking up the yard. Normally, this was her opportunity to latch onto Jason, but today she waved shyly at him and kept walking. He nodded back, as he was carrying two five gallon buckets of water to the chicken coop for Brandon. Brandon was talking his ear off, carrying the chicken feed.

"Hey Leah, come on in," I said, sounding a little more cheerful than I needed to. "I wondered when you would be back."

"Oh, yeah, I was needed at home. Helping clean up the storm," she said sheepishly, looking at her feet. "You know how it is."

I did all too well. My heart hurt for her. I was a lousy friend, and I knew it. I was overwhelmed with guilt, and more than once I tried to tell her about my kisses with Jason. But I didn't know how. There was no way she would take the news well. Instead, I said nothing, like a coward.

We gathered out floaties and headed to the pond. Leah was not one to keep secrets, and she wasted no time bringing Jason up. "So, I asked Jason out the other day," she said.

I felt my face turn red, and I knew it was not from the sun. "And?" I asked, my heart pounding in my chest.

Leah rolled her eyes. "Ugh. We were talking and laughing and so I asked him when he was going to ask me out. He got all quiet and weird, and so then I just told him he should take me on a date. He said he was sorry, but he couldn't date me because his heart belonged to someone else."

My heart was pounding so fast I could hear it in my ears. I scooped some water into my hands and started putting it on my face, shoulders and arms, trying to cool off.

"Like, who is he going to find to date that is better than me?" Leah continued. "So, I asked him if this chick was from around here, if it was someone I knew. He just shrugged and said he didn't want to get into it. I think we should find this bitch and see what I'm up against."

So, she didn't take this rejection lightly. I should have figured that. There was no way I could tell her then. This was the first time I have ever kept a secret from my best friend. I felt awful about it. But if I told her, she would never speak to me again. Our friendship meant too much to me to ruin it over a boy. I didn't even know where this was all heading, how could I have expected Leah to understand? I tried to brush this off as best I could, hoping she would just let it go. "Oh, I wouldn't give it much more thought. There are plenty of other guys around here you can date. What about Andy Johnson? You really liked him last year. He doesn't live too far from here, and I think he was into you, too."

"He's in high school," Leah rolled her eyes. "He's way too immature for me. So where does Jason go when he is done for the day? Who is he hanging out with? I have never seen him anywhere outside of this farm."

"I have no idea. He has never said, and I have never asked." This was true. Aside from him taking care of his grandparents' place, he never did mention what he did outside of the farm. Leah wasn't the only one curious about Jason's life outside of Chokecherry.

"Well, we need to find out. I have an idea, maybe you should ask him for me when you two milk," she suggested.

"I'm not getting in the middle of it, Leah. I'm sorry." Leah's obsession had to end sooner or later, and I tried to stop this whole crusade before it even started. There was no way I was going to ride around with Leah, stalking Jason, just to see who this mysterious girl was. Sadly, it was because I already knew. What was worse, was that I knew and could never tell her.

***

What used to be my least favorite chore was now my absolute favorite. But doing anything was exciting when I was with Jason. We spent our few short hours together getting to know each other, as well as fitting in some flirting and a lot more kissing. The more I learned about him, the more I liked him, and the harder it was to pry ourselves away, once milking was done.

I was curious about Jason's life before he moved to Grey Eagle. Jason couldn't remember where they lived or how many times they moved, but he spent the past four years at Fort Bragg in Fayetteville, North Carolina. Before that, he spent two years at Fort Buchanan, in San Juan, Puerto Rico.

Life on the base was lonely. Jason had a tough time making friends. Kids came and went and switching schools every few years was difficult. He was teased a lot in school, and eventually he stopped trying to make friends altogether and spent most of his time alone. Once he turned sixteen, his parents bought him his rusty Chevy pickup and he got a job on a nearby farm, milking cows. On his rare days off, he would drive to the Outer Banks and surf or sit on a pier and fish. Jason contemplated dropping out of school, but he knew how much it meant to his mother, so he stuck it out. He graduated on the B Honor Roll, had a celebratory dinner with his parents, and he left for Minnesota the next morning.

And now, he was here, with his arms around my waist, kissing me.

"I wanna take you on a date, Macy," he said as he kissed my forehead. "I want to spend more time with you, outside of this stinky parlor."

"I wish that could happen, but I don't see how," I groaned.

"Is this about Leah?" Jason asked. "Just tell her about us already. If she was any kind of friend at all, she would be happy for you."

"It's partly Leah," I sighed. "She's not going to take it well, trust me. Right now, I'm more worried about my Mom. If she finds out, she will forbid this from going any further. I don't want to take the chance. Not yet. Not now."

"Well, then we will just have to be more careful, won't we?" he mused. "What if we went to the drive-in in Long Prairie this Saturday night? You could tell your parents that you are going with Leah."

I thought about it for a minute. The idea was so appealing, and my Mother wouldn't suspect a thing. But was lying to her the right answer? "Ok," I decided. "I'll ask Mom tonight." When I looked in Jason's eyes, my hesitation melted away. Maybe one little white lie wouldn't hurt, not this one time.

Asking my Mother was more challenging than I anticipated. I waited until we were preparing supper, knowing that she would be preoccupied. I was stirring a pot of gravy while she was mashing potatoes. I wiped my sweaty hand off on my shorts. I wanted to get this over with before Brandon, Dad, and Nana came in. I didn't have the courage to outright lie to all of them. Actually, the more people I lied to, the more likely one of them would figure it out.

I took a deep breath. "Can I go to the drive-in with Leah Saturday night?"

"The drive-in, huh? It's been a long time since I have been there. Who is going to be there?" she asked.

"Wendy and Mary Beth called Leah last night and asked if we could join them," I blurted out, feeling my cheeks turning red.

"I suppose that would be fine," she finally decided.

"But you will be up and on time for church on Sunday."

"Yes, ma'am," I said. Two more days, and I would be going on my very first date, with the only boy I'd ever cared about—if Mom didn't figure it out first.

***

It took three outfit changes before I settled on jeans and a blue sweater. I tamed my hair with a flat iron and put my makeup in my purse to put on later, knowing that Mom would not let me leave the house wearing any products on my face.

Mother and Nana were sitting on the front porch, reading scriptures and swatting at mosquitoes, when I left. "I'll see you guys later," I said as I headed to my car, careful not to make eye contact.

"Where are you off to?" Nana hollered from the rocking chair.

I turned back to answer. "I'm off to a movie with some friends!"

"Good for you, dear. You deserve to have some fun. Drive safe." Nana yelled back with a wave. When I glanced over at Mom, she sat in her rocking chair, frowning. She didn't like that I was heading out this late in the evening. Could she sense that I was lying to her?

I had just enough time to apply my make-up when Jason pulled into the parking lot at the public access on Birch Lake. Although Jason wanted me to meet his grandparents, we needed to wait until the time was right. The McNally's were acquaintances of my folks, and until they found out about us, there was no use involving anyone else. Gossip flew through small towns, and it would not be out of the ordinary for one of them to say something to my parents when they saw them in town or in church. There was no telling what Mom would do if she found out about us from someone else. Most likely she would fire Jason and forbid me to ever see him again. I shuddered at the thought.

Jason wore jeans and a t-shirt—without any holes, cowboy boots and a baseball hat. As I scooted closer to the middle of the seat in his pickup, I caught a whiff of his cologne. He was sexier than I predicted he would be, and my attraction to him was growing.

"You look stunning, Macy," Jason said, studying me.

I blushed and tried to brush the compliment off. "You just think that because I am not wearing my boots that are covered in manure."

"Well, you do smell better," he laughed. "Did your parents say anything when you left?"

"No, but I feel terrible about lying to them," I admitted.

"Me, too," Jason said. "I don't know why your Mother hates me so much. I haven't done anything wrong."

"It's not you, Jason. She hates everyone," I joked. But he wasn't laughing back. "In all seriousness, she just doesn't like change. She knows you work hard on our farm. She will come around, and when she does, then we will tell her about us. And we won't have to hide or sneak around. My Mother just has this vision of how my life should be, and I think she will need some time to realize that you are becoming an important part of it."

"How exactly, does she expect your life to be?" he asked flatly.

"I suppose she dreams what every Mother would for their daughter. She wants me to go to college, get a job, marry a rich man, and start having babies. She wants me to move out of Grey Eagle, but not to live so far away that she feels she can't control my life or have a part in it. But that's her dream, not mine." This conversation was getting too serious for our first date.

Jason was somber for a minute. "Is that what you want? To have your Mom plan out your whole life for you?"

"What I want, right this minute, is to be with you, enjoying this movie." We pulled into the drive-in. The lot was nearly full, and after grabbing a bag of popcorn and a large soda to share, we pulled into the last open spot in the far back.

As the movie started, we were no longer thinking about my Mother or the future she planned. Instead, we spent the entire movie focusing on exploring each other's bodies. His body pressed tightly against mine, I could feel how much he wanted to be with me. It was almost as much as I wanted to be with him. I was falling in love, and I was powerless to stop it.

***

The lies only got easier as time went on. Mom never suspected a thing with the movie, and she never doubted that I was with anyone other than Leah. She had yet to discover that Jason and I were together, and although her hatred towards him was waning, I didn't want to give her a reason for that to change. Our relationship was still too new, and I didn't want to jeopardize it.

So, we stayed quiet, truly believing that we had everyone fooled. It was exhilarating, having this secret that no one knew about. We started sneaking around all over the place. We went to a few drive-ins, went for ice cream, we even went fishing once. But that wasn't enough. We wanted to see more of each other, so we started meeting at Willow's Pond in the evenings. We didn't have to hide at the pond or worry about who would see us and run to my Mother.

My routine stayed much the same during the day— milking cows, doing household chores, spending the afternoon with Leah at the pond, and coming home to help with dinner. After dinner, I grabbed a book, and would either read on the front porch the days we didn't meet or tell Mom I was going to read at the pond. Many nights we sat on the front porch with Nana, reading scriptures, so there were times we planned to meet, and I could never make it. Jason would wait twenty minutes, and if I was a no-show, he left.

We were meeting at the pond three to four evenings a week by late July. Jason always brought a blanket and bug spray. Sometimes the bug spray wasn't enough, and we were chased away by mosquito's. Other times we stayed until it was almost dark. It was there where we made love for the first time, and afterward we lay in each other's arms, and Jason whispered in my ear that he loved me. It was the first time for both of us. Our love making was awkward and wonderful all at the same time, and as I gazed back at him, I knew that I would cherish these moments with him forever.

The next morning, Jason beat me to the parlor and had started milking without me. He looked remorseful when I walked in.

"Are you okay? I hope last night didn't change anything between us?"

I smiled. "I'm just fine. We're just fine."

"I couldn't sleep last night, wondering what you were thinking. Like maybe you weren't ready. And when you were late this morning…" he never finished his thought.

His sincerity was so sweet that I had to bite my lip. I threw my arms around his neck. "Last night was perfect, and I've never slept better." Jason leaned in for a kiss.

"You've got me, Macy Reilly. Right where you want me."

"We've got each other," I whispered back, nuzzling his neck.

Neither one of us heard the door open. It was hard to tell how long we were standing there kissing, before we realized that we were not alone. When I looked up Leah was standing in the doorway, with her hands on her hips, and all the color had drained from her face.

"What the hell is this?" she hissed.

"Leah, it's not what it looks like," I said, taking a leap back.

"Actually, Leah, it is. And we have wanted to tell you for a long time," Jason said.

"A long time? How long is a long time? How long has this been going on? You know what," she said, shaking her head. "I don't even want to know." She turned and fled.

I ran after her. "Leah! Leah!" I shouted. "Please stop. Listen to me."

Leah turned to face me. She had tears in her eyes and her lips were trembling. "How could you do this to me, Macy? You knew how much I liked him. You *knew*, and you never said a word."

"Please, Leah," I begged. "Please hear me out. It wasn't like that. It just…sorta happened. I wanted to tell you so many times, but I didn't want to hurt you. Not like this."

"Hmm, not like this," Leah repeated. "Funny,

there were plenty of other ways you could have told me, instead of me walking in and finding the two of you making out!"

"Leah, you're my best friend," I wept, tears flowing down my cheeks. "Please, don't let this ruin us."

Leah laughed bitterly. "Best friends, huh? You made a fool out of me, Macy. I can only imagine how many times the two of you were laughing at me behind my back. You knew exactly how I felt about him, yet that didn't matter at all. You went after him anyway. Does that sound like a best friend to you? How could you, of all people, do this to me?" I was taken back by the tone in her voice and the hurt in her eyes. The hurt that I caused.

"We've never done that, Leah. Not once, not ever. You have to believe me," I cried.

Leah shook her head. "Well, it looks like I now know who his heart belongs to. Thank you, Macy, for making me out to be a total and utter fool. So long."

"Wait, Leah. Please. We need to talk about this," I pleaded, but it was useless. Leah walked away, and she had no interest in hearing what I had to say.

I watched her until I could no longer see her, hoping that she would turn around and we could work this out, the way best friends should. When she didn't, I dried my eyes and turned around. That's when I noticed Dad, tucked into the shade of the open shed, wiping his hands on an old oil rag. When our eyes met, I realized he had heard the whole thing.

Chapter 11

Macy

April 2014
Grey Eagle, Minnesota

Nana's cabin started to feel a little more like home, after I had been there for a few days. However, there wasn't much for entertainment. Although there were a few good books to choose from on the bookshelf, I couldn't concentrate. Too restless to fight my way through one, I found a bucket and some cleaner from under the sink and decided that the cabin could use a good cleaning.

I started in the kitchen, scrubbing both the inside and outside of the cabinets, and wiping down the dust encrusted dishes. Nana used to say that cleaning was good for the soul, and I never believed her. I didn't enjoy cleaning, but it gave me something to do to pass the time. Seth and the girls would be staying at the cabin when they came for the funeral, and I knew Ella and Bree would be disgusted at both the mildew smell and the old interior.

As much as I ached for my girls, I was glad that they weren't here to witness my emotional rollercoaster. This trip opened wounds in me that had long ago healed, or so I thought. I did my best to bury the past and to distance myself from anyone who was a part of it, and even I could see how wrong that was. It didn't take long for me to realize exactly what I missed all these years from Chokecherry. Sadly, I could never get back the years I missed with my family, but I hoped, in time, that Brandon would forgive me. Would my father have forgiven me? Perhaps, I would never know. And that guilt would haunt me forever.

As I started scrubbing the fridge, I thought of my Mother, and how we never got past what happened. Even all these years later, I don't know that I would have ever been able to forgive her, and I doubt that she would have ever forgiven me. There had been too high a price to pay, and no amount of time or distance would ever change that.

Our relationship had never been great from the start. She didn't know how to be anything other than strict, with set rules and regulations. My mistake embarrassed her deeply, and she would never forget it. Knowing our relationship was beyond repair; I moved as far away from Chokecherry Farm as I could. Even California felt too close sometimes.

Once I left for college in Chicago, I never looked back—not even when Dad called me five years ago to let me know Mom was diagnosed with breast cancer. Instead of trying to repair our relationship, I did the complete opposite. I rarely called, and when I did, it was tense. Our conversations were over before they began, and they never ended well. I'm not proud to admit it, but I thought she deserved it after all that had transpired between us.

Our final phone call came a few days before her death. That's when it hit me that Mom was really dying. There's not much you can say to someone who is dying that you spent almost fifteen years despising. I realized during our last conversation that that wasn't how I wanted it to end. Like every other regret in my life, that epiphany came too little, too late.

"I'm sorry I could never be the daughter you wanted me to be." I had told her.

"Don't say that…you were everything…I ever wanted." She panted, struggling to get the words out. "I hope you know…I tried to do…what was best…for you."

I bit my tongue, knowing that this was not the time to be spiteful. This was the closest thing to an apology that I was going to get. I needed to take it or leave it. I decided to take it.

"I know. I'm sorry for, well, for everything that happened." Damn the tears that started falling. "I'm sorry you are sick. I'm sorry…that I wasn't there. I love you, Mom."

"I love…you…too," Mom said, the exhaustion in her voice was evident that this conversation was taking a toll on her. "Tell my…girls…that I…love them."

"I will," I promised.

She died two days later. Seth and I flew in the day of the wake and stayed for the funeral the next morning. We flew back to California that evening, as Seth was working on another high-profile divorce case. The girls were too young to travel, so they stayed with Elvira. My Father was beyond disappointed at our short visit. Brandon didn't look my way once.

That was the last time I came home, and now, five years later, I was back as Dad was in his final hours. Never did I think that I would be here, scrubbing the floors on my hands and knees at Nana's cabin, getting ready for a longer stay. Best guess was I could be here at least another week or so, depending on when Dad passed and how soon the services would happen.

Maybe there was a silver lining in all of this. Brandon and I were getting along better than ever, joking and hurling slight insults at one another. Brandon took everything in stride. He never pushed me or asked questions. But soon, Brandon and I were going to have to hash out the past. All I could do was cross my fingers and pray that I didn't lose him in this process too. I couldn't bear the thought of losing him. Not when we were just getting to know each other again. I had lost too much already.

The cabin smelled much better after I cleaned the kitchen and bathroom. I opened the windows and shook the rugs outside. The place reminded me of Nana – always clean, fresh, and ready for company. Oh, how I missed her…and her fresh chocolate chip cookies.

Charlotte came by the cabin when she was ready to go to the nursing home. Her Mom was watching the kids, so Charlotte could see her father in-law. She knew Brandon needed more time with him than she did, so she always volunteered to stay behind. But now that it was getting closer, she wanted to make sure she got to say her goodbye's too. She asked if we could ride together, and I agreed, although I wanted to get there much earlier.

"Wow, this place hasn't been this clean since Brandon and I lived here," Charlotte said as she stepped inside. "Howard wasn't much of a housekeeper, and he said he didn't want me here, poking around."

"That sounds like something he would say. I didn't have much else to do," I said, grabbing my purse and keys. "I thought I would clean it up some before Seth, Bree and Ella get here. The musty smell was getting to me."

"Well, if you need anything else, let me know. We could move the television from our bedroom out here, so you have something to watch. I don't want you to get bored."

"Oh, no, that's fine. I don't watch too much TV. There are plenty of books I could read. I picked out a few when I dusted them off." It was really nice not having a TV. The Prescott divorce drama had yet to die down, and I had no desire to keep hearing about it.

We waved at the kids while we pulled out of the yard. "I just want you to know that Brandon and I are so glad you decided to stay with us. We love having you here. The kids do too. I think Brandon feels like he doesn't have to face this burden alone anymore. As hard as this is, I can tell that having you here has been good for him. He has been in a better mood since you got here, even under these circumstances."

"Thank you, Charlotte. And thank you for letting me stay in the cabin. I thought it would be harder, you know, to be on the farm. But it's not. It's been..." I trailed off.

"Healing?" Charlotte finished.

"Yes, healing. I've been far too angry for far too long. I resented this place for so many years, and that was unfair. My therapist will be so proud of me. I figured this out on my own."

Charlotte laughed, and then grew serious. "I wasn't here for that period of your life and I can't imagine how hard that must have been. But we are here now, and I'd like to think that this will be the start of...being a family. Brandon needs you, Macy. And your children have cousins that they don't even know."

"This means more to me than you could ever know." I squeezed Charlotte's hand. "Bree and Ella will love your kids. I can't wait for them to meet."

Charlotte squeezed back. "Can we stop at the grocery store? I would like to pick up some flowers for Howard."

"Sure," I said, turning off my blinker and going straight instead. "I need to grab a few things too."

Charlotte and I went our separate ways at the grocery store. She headed to the flower section, and I headed for coffee. I found Nana's coffee pot while I was cleaning, and I washed it out and set it on the counter. Hopefully, the old machine still worked. I grabbed some creamer, and then headed over to get more shampoo and conditioner.

Charlotte beat me to the register. Her eyes widened, and she quickly stepped in front of the magazine rack, blocking my view.

"What's wrong?" I asked, perturbed.

"You go on ahead." Charlotte said, not willing to move.

"Is there something you don't want me to see?" I joked. The look on Charlotte's face gave it away. "What is it Charlotte?"

"Macy, please, just go ahead of me." Charlotte pleaded.

"Move. Now." Charlotte paused, and then took one side-step, shaking her head.

All eight of the magazine racks were filled with the same sleazy tabloid. I could see why Charlotte tried to stop me from seeing it. The cover page was a picture of my husband, shirtless and wearing his navy-blue swim trunks. He was rubbing sunscreen lotion on Asia Prescott's bare back, in my backyard. The caption read: 'Home-wrecker Asia Prescott's affair with her married attorney.'

I stared at Charlotte in horror. "Macy, you know how untrue these shitty tabloids are," she said. I nodded dumbly and turned away before I could buy every single one of those magazines, just to get them off the shelf. Taking a deep breath, I reminded myself that there were millions of these in print. Even if I took them off the shelf in Long Prairie, there would be millions of these, in every rural town and every big city, all over the United States.

My girls didn't deserve this. I didn't deserve this. Not in my wildest dreams did I ever think that my husband would be involved in a world of fame and fortune. Nor could I have ever predicted that I would be standing in line at a grocery store, looking at a picture of my husband rubbing lotion on a naked back on one of the most famous actresses of our generation.

My heart tightened in my chest and I tried taking a few deep breaths to keep myself in check. Instinctively, I dug around for my pill bottle in my bag. I knew I was running low on my Ativan, but right now I could have cared less. I was about to yank the bottle out of my bag, when I noticed someone buying the magazine. I looked past Charlotte to see who would want to buy such filth. When the customer looked up at the cashier to collect her change, I recognized her immediately.

It was none other than Leah Watson, my former best friend.

CHAPTER 12

JASON

APRIL 2014

INDIANAPOLIS, INDIANA

"Can I get you anything else, sir?"

I shook my head. "No, thank you."

"Thanks for stopping by. You can take care of your tab at the register." The waitress scurried over to the next table with a fresh coffee pot in hand.

I checked my watch. I had another fifteen minutes to wait for my oil change before I could hit the road. Another twelve hours to go and I would be home. I was looking forward to sleeping in my own bed and cooking my own meals. Maybe I could even get a few hours of fishing in, too.

I paid my tab and walked over to the gas station. Grabbing a few drinks and snacks, I went to the checkout. As I waited, the magazine rack caught my eye. There was a picture of a shirtless man and a woman's naked back with the caption: '*Home-wrecker Asia Prescott's affair with her married attorney.*'

Son of a bitch. I grabbed the magazine, paid, and headed out the door. I paged through it until I found the article. Growling, I crumpled the paper into a ball and whipped it into the trash can. How could that idiot do that to her?

This is none of your business, I told myself. I paced the parking lot, waiting for my semi. Not knowing what else to do, I sent Brandon a text.

Hey, Brandon. Is Macy okay? I just saw the article. I hit send before I could change my mind.

I'm not sure. Charlotte's with her at the nursing home. Dad's not doing so well. He's on hospice. Won't be much longer, Brandon responded.

I'm sorry to hear that. Can I have her number?

Sorry, man. I've been meaning to talk to her about that, but I haven't had a chance to. She's been with Dad a lot.

I'll be home soon. I'll talk to her then.

Good, Brandon said.

So, Macy was home. She never came home. Howard's condition must be bad for her to have shown up in Minnesota. Would she even want to see me after all this time? I needed to see her. I had so much to tell her. It was time to get home, and fast.

CHAPTER 13
MACY

I had a white-knuckled grip on the steering wheel as I sat in the parking lot of the nursing home, unsure of what to do next. Somehow, I managed to escape without a run-in with Leah. I purchased my items and ran out of the store as quickly as I could, before someone noticed me, or worse yet, commented on the article that would now wreak havoc on my life.

Poor Charlotte apologized profusely for even asking to stop at the grocery store at all, and she tried her best to assure me that there was never any truth to those trashy tabloids. I gripped the wheel even harder, not bothering to answer. My mind was trying to process that cover: 'Home-wrecker: Asia Prescott's affair with her married attorney.' Eventually Charlotte stopped trying to make me feel better, and we rode in silence across town to the nursing home. She grabbed her flowers and headed inside, leaving me alone.

Why would Asia Prescott want Seth? She had only been known to date the latest breakout star, or musician, and occasionally, an athlete. Seth did not fit in any category. For one, he was a happily married lawyer with two children. And two, he wasn't famous enough for her. He didn't fit the red-carpet look. Seth was certainly handsome, but he did not fit the standard for Hollywood handsome.

Would Seth really cheat on me after 15 years of marriage? The day we met, I knew I could depend on him. He was stable. His honesty drew me to him instantaneously, and I knew he would never hurt me. But sitting in this rental car, instead of with my dying father, I had some serious doubts. The picture of Asia's green bikini bottoms and tan bare back suddenly cast a dark cloud over my marriage. What did this mean for us?

Rubbing my sweaty hands on my pants, I closed my eyes and started practicing all the calming techniques my therapist preached about in our weekly sessions. Breathe in and out, in and out. After repeating this for several minutes, I decided I was put together enough to go inside. I peeked at my cell phone first, finding six missed calls from Seth. Trying to stay in control, I called him back. He answered on the first ring.

"Macy," he was out of breath. "We need to talk."

"We need to talk, huh? Do you think that maybe we should have had this conversation before I stood in line at the grocery store, looking at a picture of my husband with his hands all over another woman?" I started crying.

"Fuck! I wanted to talk to you before you saw it or heard about it. I just heard about it today, and I called as soon as I did. Macy, nothing happened. I'm not cheating on you. This is all a publicity stunt. We found out it was Augustus' photographer who took the photos."

"Oh, so there's more than one photo. That's just great. I can only imagine what other pictures will show up. What else am I going to see, Seth? What is on those photos that I should know about?"

"Damn it, Macy. You know me better than that. You know I would never do this to you. You knew that Asia was coming over to play in the pool with the kids. The only time I touched her is when I put sunscreen on her. I swear to you that that is all it was. She played with the girls for an hour or so and then she left."

"How could you do this to me?" I screamed. "Dad is dying, Seth. And while I am here watching him die, you are feeling up Asia Prescott. You were rubbing your hands all over her naked back—in front of my girls! I should have known something was going on. As soon as I am out of town, the first thing she does is make herself at home. God, I'm such an idiot."

"You have to believe me, honey. I am not cheating on you. She asked me to put on lotion, and I did, and then she swam with the girls. You know I would never do something like this. Macy, I love you."

"Well you have a funny way of showing it. I can't deal with this right now, Seth. My father is dying. I should be in there, holding his hand right now. Not sitting out here, talking to you about Asia Prescott." I choked out.

"You have to believe me, Macy. None of this is true. This is just a way for Augustus to hurt her. I'm so sorry that we got caught up in this mess. I'm done with her press junkets, so I have no reason to ever see her again. Macy, I love you, and only you. You know I would never do anything to hurt you. Ever."

I wiped my eyes with the back of my hand and looked in the mirror. Mascara ran down my cheeks. "That's what I used to believe. And now…I'm just not sure anymore. I have to go," I said. "My father needs me right now. Tell the girls I will call them later." I hung up before Seth could respond.

My hands trembled as I threw my phone back in my bag. It was hard enough being back in Grey Eagle, with my past bubbling back up, threatening to spill over any minute, and agonizing over my father's impending death. But to top it off, the newest Hollywood scandal could potentially end my marriage. How much more could I possibly handle?

Making a mental note to call my doctor to get more pills, I wiped off my mascara as best I could, and slipped on my sunglasses. I had to focus on my Dad, as impossible as it seemed. Inhaling deeply, I squared my shoulders, held my head high and walked inside the nursing home, for possibly the last time.

***

Charlotte wept unashamedly as she sat next to Dad's bed, holding his hand. Gracie was checking his blood pressure on the monitors, and then typing her notes on the computer in the corner of the room.

"Good afternoon, Mrs. Whitaker," Gracie said when I came in. "How are you doing, dear?"

"I'm okay," I replied, removing my sunglasses, revealing my puffy red eyes.

"Oh, Mrs. Whitaker, I'm so sorry. Your father was a good man, and I will miss him a great deal. I will miss his smile and all his jokes, even the dirty ones. I don't think it will be much longer, though. Maybe a few hours, at most." Gracie said, sliding a chair my way.

"Thank you, Gracie," I said, appreciating her kind words. "My father always spoke very highly of you."

Gracie beamed and squeezed my shoulder when I sat down. "Let me grab you girls some coffee."

After Gracie left, Charlotte turned to me. "Brandon is on his way. He found a neighbor to take care of the chores for the rest of today. Sandy came in here earlier and said it will happen soon."

"I don't think I am ready to say good-bye. Not yet."

"Me neither," Charlotte said.

We sat silently until Brandon got there, each of us lost in our own thoughts. Gracie stopped in several times to watch his progress and let us know his body was shutting down. Brandon and Charlotte held each other and cried, and I sat on the opposite side. We shared stories that made us laugh and cry. They did their best to make me feel included, but I knew I wouldn't have been able to lean on Seth, even if he was here. Not anymore.

Three hours later, my father, Howard Reilly, drew his final breath.

***

The wake and funeral were set up prior to Dad's passing. He planned out his funeral when Mom died, not wanting his children to make such tough decisions. Brandon and I finalized his obituary and set the funeral date. The only thing we had left to do was to get family pictures for the funeral home and church.

I spent the next two days going through the spare bedroom of Nana's cabin, pulling out boxes of pictures and some of his treasures. I put together four tag board collages, starting from the few black and white pictures of when he was a young boy, to when he and Mom starting dating, to their wedding photos. There were family photos from when we were babies all the way into the early teenage years.

The photos abruptly stopped in 1994, and other

than a few photos of Brandon and Charlotte's wedding, there were no more family photos with all our families together. Brandon and Charlotte hadn't had a family photo updated in quite a while, so Gideon and Stella were missing from their most recent photos. Our most recent family photos weren't in any of these boxes either, so Elvira packed some recent ones to send with the girls.

As I drove to the Minneapolis airport to pick up Seth and the girls, my thoughts drifted to Elvira and how much she had done for us. She stepped up without hesitation and handled everything at home, probably better than I would have. The girls did not miss one homework assignment, extra-curricular activity, or play date. She cooked, did the grocery shopping, laundry and housework. She was there when Seth wasn't. Elvira packed Seth and the girls' luggage, even adding some extra outfits, jewelry and shoes that I needed for the funeral. She had some much-needed time off for the funeral, but it was not a big enough thank you for all she did for my family. So, I phoned my travel agent and asked her to plan a vacation for Elvira to visit her family in Mexico.

I made it to the airport about twenty minutes early. It felt like it had been years since I had seen the girls, but it wasn't even a full week. Pacing the baggage claim, I stared at the monitors to make sure there were not any delays. I had only spoken with Seth once over the phone since our fight, which was just to let him know that Dad had passed away. He didn't bring up Asia, but it was obvious that she was on both of our minds. Since then, I only communicated with Seth via text to plan for their arrival time.

The girls shrieked when they saw me, took off running and jumped into my arms, almost knocking me over. Seth trailed slowly behind, carrying a backpack and a carry-on suitcase.

"Oh, my beautiful girls, I missed you so much," I said, hugging them both tightly. "I want to hear everything I missed while I have been away."

"You didn't miss a thing," said Bree. "I've been bored."

"It hasn't been boring," Ella said. "We got to go swimming with Asia Prescott! She is so much fun, Mom. She is such a good swimmer and she said she would take me scuba diving."

"Scuba diving, huh? We'll see about that," I said, glancing up at Seth. He was staring at me, unsure of what to say. Before he could lean in for a hug, I grabbed the girls' hands and headed over to baggage claim. Bree yanked her hand out of mine.

"Mom, seriously," she said. "I am not a baby."

"When I left town you were only eleven, and now you're what…at least sixteen? How did that happen in a week?" I mused, ruffling her hair. Bree rolled her eyes and crossed her arms.

"Next week she'll be leaving for college," Seth said, trying to lighten the mood.

"I hope we have longer than a week," I said, smiling at Bree. I could not bring myself to look Seth in the eye, but I didn't want the girls to notice the tension between us.

Bree scowled, and not bothering to answer us, she pulled her suitcase off the ramp. We followed suit, and soon were back on the highway, with a two-hour drive looming ahead of us.

"Does our hotel have a swimming pool?" Ella asked.

"We aren't staying in a hotel, honey. We are staying in my Nana's cabin, which is out on Brandon and Charlotte's farm."

"We are staying on a stinkin' *farm*? In a *cabin*?" Bree wrinkled her nose and pouted.

"Yes, Bree, we are. It's where I grew up. You'll like it out there," I said to assure her.

"No, I won't." She huffed and stared out the window.

"Well, I'm sorry to hear that. There should be something you can find out there to do. I always did as a child. And you have four cousins to meet. They are so excited to meet you both." I watched in the rearview mirror as Bree put on her headphones and leaned her head against the window.

"I can't wait to meet them!" Ella said as she copied Bree and put on her headset.

I turned the radio on and flipped through a few stations. I could feel Seth glancing my way, and I fought the urge to look back at him. Instead, I kept my eyes on the road and stayed silent, determined not to break the ice first. Images of Asia's perfect bare back and toned butt burned my mind, and I couldn't quite get past it. I still didn't know how far their relationship went, and what that now meant for us.

"Macy," Seth started.

"Shhh," I said, glancing in the rearview mirror. "This is not the time to talk about this."

"I know," he said. "But I haven't been able to eat or sleep. We need to talk about this."

I sighed. "Yeah, you're right."

"When? After we go home?" Seth asked.

"I don't know if I will be going home when you guys do. I need to clean out Dad's room at the nursing home and I should probably finish packing up his things in the cabin. It's been torn apart getting everything ready for this funeral. So, I guess we should figure this out tonight. After Dad's wake."

"There is nothing to figure out, Macy. Like I already told you, nothing happened. It was just a stupid picture. Asia feels terrible about it."

My hands gripped the steering wheel. "I'm sure she does," I growled.

Seth sighed and shook his head. Neither of us spoke again until we pulled into Chokecherry farm.

***

The funeral home in Grey Eagle had enough room for about seventy-five people. The wake was from five until eight, and even before five o'clock came, folks were already piling in the door, ready to pay their respects.

Seth gave me the space I needed and kept an eye on the girls as they played with Brandon and Charlotte's children. The kids became fast friends and more than once Seth had to scold them for shrieking and running around. Fortunately, Charlotte's Mom came right away to pay her respects and to take their kids home with her.

There was a steady stream of visitors. Members from my parents' church stopped by, co-workers who worked with my Mother at the bank, and several neighbors, friends and community members. Many relatives also came from all over Minnesota as well.

As the evening dragged on, it became increasingly clear that this wake would not be over by eight. Brandon and I stood in the front, next to my Father's lifeless body, greeting all visitors with either hugs or handshakes. Countless stories and memories were shared, and thankfully most of them were entertaining and light-hearted. But when I checked to see how long the line still was, I noticed Leah Watson and her parents were standing in line.

My mind went blank, bile rose in my throat. I swallowed hard, hoping I wouldn't cause an embarrassing scene. I hadn't talked to Leah in twenty years, and after seeing her buy the tabloid featuring my husband, I highly doubted I would want to talk to her now. But here she was, standing in line with her parents, and I had just a few moments before we would be face to face.

Seth tapped me on the shoulder, drawing me out of my panicked state. I spun around quickly.

"The girls are getting tired. Mind if we head back to the cabin?" Seth asked, checking his watch. "It's already 8:30."

I looked over at the girls sitting on the pew bench. Ella was leaning her head on Bree's shoulder, exhausted.

"Yes, thank you. This should be wrapping up soon." But as I peeked at the entrance, I saw several more people enter. "I'll ride home with Brandon and Charlotte. We will have to pack up these flowers and picture boards and bring them to the church yet tonight."

Seth leaned in and kissed me on the forehead. "I'll see you soon, dear."

I gave the girls a kiss and a hug goodnight. They left willingly. By the time I got back in my place near the coffin, the Watson's were next in line.

Leah's parents hugged me first and told me what a great neighbor and friend my parents had been to them over the years, and how much they were going to miss him. I appreciated their sentiments. I realized how much I missed them, and how much things had changed since high-school.

Leah leaned in for an awkward hug. "I'm sorry for your loss. Howard was a great man," she said, looking at the ground. She twirled her hair through her fingers, which only happened when she was flirting or when she was nervous.

"Thank you," I said curtly.

"So…how have you been?" she asked.

"It's been a difficult week," I answered. For more than one reason, I wanted to add, but I knew I didn't have to. Leah was up to date on all my misfortunes lately.

The years hadn't been too kind to Leah, either. Charlotte informed me that she was in an ugly divorce with her third husband. She had two kids from her first marriage who lived with their father. Leah struggled with alcohol for many years, and there was speculation that she may have been involved with drugs too. She had been in and out of treatment facilities, and she was staying with her parents since she was struggling to find a job.

She had definitely aged. Her blonde scraggly hair was fried from years of cheap hair dye, and her dark roots were a good four inches long. She was wearing worn out jeans and an oversized black hooded sweatshirt. When her eyes met mine, all I saw was emptiness. Like the rest of us, she had battled her own demons. Unfortunately, she wasn't strong enough to fight off her ghosts.

"Macy, I have tried so many times over the years to reach out to you. I have wanted to apologize to you for so long. I…I should have been a better friend."

"Water under the bridge," I lied with a shrug. "We were young, and it was a long time ago. I've moved on."

"I'm glad, Macy. I really am. How long are you in town? Do you think we could grab a cup of coffee or meet for lunch before you go? I'd love to catch up,"

Leah asked, twirling her hair again.

"I'm not sure. I will be here a couple more days, and then I'll be heading back to Los Angeles. If I can fit it in, should I call you at your parents?"

"That'd mean a lot, Macy." Leah looked hopeful. She hugged me a little tighter, and then she moved on to pay her respects to Brandon.

Twenty years later, Leah Watson actually apologized to me. I never thought that day would come. I neither expected it nor could have prepared myself for it. Maybe this was another one of those silver lining moments. Could I make peace with Leah? Too much time had passed for us to ever be friends again, and we lived worlds away. Would it even pay to catch up before I went home? What if she hadn't changed at all? Maybe all she wanted was to meet to discuss Seth and Asia Prescott.

I mulled this over while I packed up the flowers and cards. Brandon and Charlotte were quietly speaking with the funeral home owners in a small office. While I was boxing everything up, I caught a scent that wasn't from the flowers and I instantly froze. I would know that citrusy, musky smell anywhere. I didn't hear anyone come in, but I knew I wasn't alone.

When I turned around, I stood face to face with one of my ghosts. It was Jason McNally, the father of my first-born child.

CHAPTER 14

MACY

Leah still wasn't speaking to me. She refused to answer my calls, and twice I walked over there to talk to her in person. The first time she never answered the door, and the second time her parents said she was up in her room feeling under the weather. What should have been my happiest summer was tainted by the fact that my best friend wanted nothing to do with me. It hurt like hell.

I replayed our fight over and over. I should have done things differently. I should have been honest and told her right away that Jason and I were together. But I didn't want to hurt her. I didn't want her to be mad or jealous or feel left out, which didn't matter anyways because, in the end, that's exactly what happened. It had been a month, and she still hadn't forgiven me. Jason and I both figured that she would have come around by now, and that our friendship would have picked up right where it left off.

Oddly enough, Dad never told Mom about us. Many nights, I crept over to the heating vent in the upstairs hallway to listen in on my parents. While I

98

listened to Mom berate Jason and beg Dad to let him go, he never relented. Our secret seemed to be safe with him, and the three of us kept on pretending that nothing was going on.

But spending quality time with Jason was getting harder. Now that my father knew that Leah and I weren't speaking, I couldn't keep lying to Mom and telling her that I was going out with Leah. Dad wouldn't stand for it. He would know that I was sneaking out with Jason. Although he said nothing about it, I didn't know how he would feel if he knew we were going out on real dates as a real couple. I was certain he didn't know about our secret meetings out at the pond. Our dates stopped abruptly, except for our minimal outings at Willow's Pond. I still alternated between bringing my empty journal or a book, and some nights I skipped going all together so that no one would suspect anything. I never gave lying a second thought anymore.

"Can I ask you something?" I asked one night at the pond. We were cuddled in a blanket after just making love. It was sunset, and there was enough of a breeze to keep the mosquito's at bay, at least for the time being.

"Anything," Jason said.

"Why me? I mean, why would you rather be with someone like me, instead of someone like…Leah?" The question had plagued me since the moment he kissed me.

"Leah is beautiful, Macy. No one can dispute that. But she is also brazen, bossy, superficial, and she is a horrible friend. If she can't get what she wants, then no one can. She's too jealous to be happy for anyone, especially you. Honestly, I can't stand those types of people. She always had to be the center of attention. I don't have the time or energy for that."

"She's not a horrible friend…" I started.

"Yes, she is. She should be supporting you, not mad at you because you have a boyfriend." He kissed the top of my head. "The day I picked you up on the side of the road, I knew I wanted to know more about you. I thought I hit the jackpot when I realized my interview was at your farm."

I leaned up and kissed him. "I love you."

"I love you, too. But now I need to ask you something."

"Go for it," I said.

"When are you going to tell your Mom about us?"

I swallowed hard and shrugged unhappily. "I don't know. If she finds out about us, she will end it. You will be fired, and we will never get to see each other again. If we can just make it through my senior year, then we can be together, and no one can stop us, not even my Mother."

"You want to wait a whole year to tell her?" he sat up and gathered his clothing. "We are supposed to hide this for a whole year? So, I can't take my girlfriend on a date, or go to her prom. Instead, we just keep sneaking around out here until the mosquito's chase us away?"

"What do you want me to do, Jason? It's this or nothing. It can't be both. My Mother will forbid me to see you, do you get that? Don't you know how scared I am every single day that she will find out about us? Do you think that's what I want?" I finished dressing and started folding the blankets.

"You're only thinking about right now," Jason's voice softened. "What about when school starts, and we can't milk together anymore? Then all we have is this pond until it's too cold to be out here. Then what, we don't see each other all winter?"

I paused. "So, you think if she knows about us that she will be okay with it and she will let us see each other, is that it? Do you think she is going to encourage this relationship? Even when she finds out I have been lying to her for months?"

"I don't know," Jason shook his head. "But maybe, the sooner she knows, the sooner she will get used to the idea. She might try to stop us at first, but over time she will come around. We will just have to follow her rules until she lightens up. Your Dad doesn't seem to mind that we are together."

I shook my head. "Dad doesn't know the extent of it. And you don't know my Mother like I do, Jason. You don't know what she is capable of." The only time we ever argued or disagreed on anything was over Leah or my Mother, and I hated it. I wrapped my arms around him and buried my face in his chest. "I'm scared to tell her. I'm not ready for this to end."

"It doesn't have to," he said, squeezing me back. "But there is a lot to think about. What about next year when you go off to college? Where are you going to go?"

Originally, I had planned to move as far away as I could, just to have some breathing room. But now there was Jason. "I'll go where ever you'll be. I can go to a community college around here. There are colleges in Saint Cloud, Alexandria, Brainerd, and Willmar. I can find somewhere close."

"But Macy, that's not what I want for you. I don't want you to feel stuck because of me. I can't leave my grandparents. They need a caretaker and they refuse to go to a nursing home. I can't just leave them. But I'm not going to let you settle, just so we can be together. You have bigger dreams that can't be found in Grey Eagle."

"My dream is being with you, right here, right now," I said, wondering if he was breaking up with me. "We can figure out the rest when the time comes. Can't we?"

Jason sighed and broke away from me. "I better get going. It's getting dark and your parents will be looking for you soon." He took his blankets and headed towards his pickup truck.

"I love you," I called out to him. He never responded.

***

Although our conversation weighed heavily on my mind, I still believed that no good could come from Mom finding out about us. But Jason was right, school was fast approaching. And once it started, it would damn near be impossible for us to spend time together. The idea of not seeing Jason every day made my stomach clench. I never wanted this summer to end.

"What's got you in such a state, dear?" Nana asked one afternoon after I unpacked her groceries from the car.

"Nothing," I mumbled, wiping the sweat off my forehead with my tank top. The heat peaked at a hundred degrees and it wasn't even noon. Nana didn't like the air conditioner running for too long, and today was no exception.

"Let me get you some lemonade and some fresh cookies. I bet they are still warm. Sit down, dear."

I sat down immediately. It was hard to breathe in here. Nana set a plate of cookies and a mason jar in front of me.

"Now, tell me what's bothering you dear," she pried.

I shook my head. "I'm fine."

"Oh, I see. It must be trouble in paradise. Did you and Jason break up?"

I nearly spat out my drink. "What? I mean, how did you know about us?"

Nana's eyes sparkled. "I know summer love when I see it. I've seen how you two look at each other. You are both smitten."

My face flushed. I thought we had been so careful. "I didn't realize we were being so obvious."

Nana laughed. "Don't fret, dear. Your secret is safe with me. I am assuming that you aren't spending all that time at the pond alone. Am I right?"

"Nana!" I choked, wiping the lemonade off my face.

"I'm no fool. So, let's get to the bottom of it. Are you two having a quarrel?"

I smiled. "Not exactly. Jason thinks I should tell Mom about us. But I know what will happen if I do. She isn't going to like it, and she won't let us see each other anymore."

Nana frowned. "She really doesn't like that young man."

"I don't know why. Everyone else likes him and he is a hard worker. I don't know why she hates him. Now everything will change when I start school. We won't get to milk together except on weekends, and soon, we won't be able to see each other at the pond. It will get too cold."

Nana sighed. "That is quite the predicament. I'm sure you will both find a way to make it work if you really want it to. Well, she's not going to hear about this from me, dear. But I would recommend telling her before she finds this out from someone else. If she is the last to know about this, shit's really going to hit the fan."

***

With school a week away, I finally decided that I had to tell Mom that Jason and I were a couple. Although I still had my reservations, I knew Jason was right. Once school was in full swing, we would never see each other unless we had my parents blessing. Maybe she would come around after the initial shock wore off. Maybe Dad could talk some sense into her. I couldn't keep lying to her anymore. It was time to come clean.

For almost three months I had been lying non-stop and it was time to end it. The lies were so easy that I had no problem looking my Mother straight in the eye while I was doing it. She still had no clue that Leah hadn't been here in over a month. I always had an excuse or reason why she had to leave early or couldn't come that day. Mom figured she had finally gotten over her disgusting crush on Jason and stopped throwing herself at him. This pleased her so much that she started asking about her less and less.

Jason supported me as best he could, but I was a disaster. My nerves were making me feel sick, and I wasn't sure if I should try to vomit to make myself feel better, or if I was going to get hit with a sudden bout of diarrhea. The prognosis was grim for both circumstances. My chest tightened, and at times, breathing became difficult. So, this is what a heart attack feels like, I thought. Maybe I would drop dead before I had to tell her.

Much to my dismay, I was still very much alive when she pulled into the yard. It was now or never. Everyone seemed to have disappeared, and I didn't know if that would work in my favor or not.

Mom stood on the porch with her hands on her hips, watching me walk up to the house. Her lips were pressed tightly together, and her eyes narrowed.

"Hi, Mom," I stammered. She seemed pissed about something.

"You'll never guess who came into the bank today," she said, her hands still on her hips.

"Who?" I asked.

"Leah. And guess what she had to tell me?" she hissed.

Shit. I stared at the porch floor. I felt my chest, neck and face turn beet red. I felt the vomit rise to the back of my throat.

"She told me what a disloyal friend you have been. That poor girl had tears streaming down her face. She told me that you have been sneaking around here with Jason behind her back when you knew she was in love with him."

Tears sprang to my eyes and I shook my head. "No…" I whispered.

"No? So, you're telling me she is lying? Tell me that you haven't been sneaking around here with that loser. Look at me!" she yelled.

I gathered up what courage I had and met her eyes. "It's not like that, Mom."

"Are you, or are you not, seeing that boy?" she loomed over me.

"I am," I whispered, trying not to shake.

"Like hell you are!" she yelled, grabbing my shoulders and shaking me. "Listen here and listen good. I am only going to say this once. You will never, ever see that boy again. Do you understand me?"

"But, Mom, if you let me explain…"

"No, let me explain, Macy Reilly. You are never to see that boy again. Ever. You think that you can just lie to me and get away with it? You've got another thing coming. Leah told me everything you've been hiding from us. You weren't going out with her or any other friend. You were sneaking around with that low life behind our backs."

A sob caught in my throat. "Mom, please," I begged.

Her nails dug into my shoulders. "This ends now!" she screamed.

Dad, Brandon, Jason and Nana came rushing over to see what was going on. Mother let go of her grip on me and I absentmindedly started rubbing my burning shoulders.

"Elaine!" Dad yelled. "What the hell is going on?"

Mom crossed her arms and smirked. "What's going on? I'll tell you what's going on. It appears your hired help has been sneaking around with our daughter. They have been hiding this little so-called relationship for months. I happened to find out the truth at work today. Thank goodness I did, or who knows how long these lies would have lasted."

We all froze, unsure of what to say. I kept wiping away the tears. Mother huffed. "Aren't you going to say something, Howard?"

Dad cleared his throat. "I think we should all sit down and have a civilized conversation about this."

Mom rolled her eyes. "Oh, that's not necessary. Jason, you are fired. Do not ever show up here again, or I will make sure that no one in a hundred-mile radius will ever hire you to work on their farm."

"Elaine, you do not get to make this decision for me. It's almost chopping season, and I need him here. He's staying," Dad said firmly.

"Oh, so you are telling me that you are okay with this?" she shrieked. "Wait, did you know about this, Howard?"

I looked over at Jason and gave him the 'I told you so' look. He shrugged.

"I did," Dad said, squaring his shoulders.

"I see," Mom turned around and walked into the house, letting the screen door slam behind her.

For the first time in my life, Dad was standing up to Mom, although I wished it wasn't on my account. He may end up regretting it later, but for now he seemed confident in his decision. Mother was definitely out for revenge now.

Nana headed back to the cabin, and Brandon headed over to the garden to finish weeding.

"Alright, guys," Dad looked at us and pinched the bridge of his nose. "This is going to get ugly for a while. No more sneaking around. No more dates. No more make out sessions in the parlor or flirting all day long. I'm not saying that you have to break up, but for now, just cool it until this whole thing blows over."

"Yes, sir," Jason said as I nodded.

"That's settled then. Brandon will be joining your morning milkings until school starts. Jason, let's have you out of here before Elaine gets home each day. It's about the only way you are going to get to keep your job, if you still want one here."

"Yes, I do. Thank you." Jason sighed in relief.

"You better get going then," Dad said. "Before all hell breaks loose again."

Jason didn't need to be told twice. He gave me a small smile and headed over to his pickup truck.

I collapsed on the porch swing, confused. We hadn't fooled anyone except Mom, and we thought we were so careful. Hopefully no one saw what we were doing at the pond, but I couldn't think about that now. I couldn't understand why being with Jason was that big of a deal. Why couldn't Leah and Mom be happy for me? What did this mean for our future?

CHAPTER 15
MACY

The drive to Long Prairie on the first day of school was incredibly lonely. There had been only a handful of times that I drove alone since I got my license. I didn't bother calling Leah to see if she needed a ride, even though I debated it. I told myself, if she needed a ride, she would have contacted me by now. She could ride the school bus for all I cared.

I never thought I would look forward to going back to school, but after this last week I needed the reprieve. Things had only gotten worse at home. I listened as my parents fought each night about Jason and me, and I didn't even have to listen near the vent. The fighting was so loud it reached my bedroom.

Mom was still giving us the silent treatment. I tried to have dinner nearly finished each day before she came home, just so we wouldn't have to spend more time together than necessary. Other than the clinking of the silverware, our dinners were silent. Even Nana refrained from her usual small talk and jokes.

Not even Leah's deception or the fallout with

108

Mom changed how I felt about Jason. Now, more than ever, I wanted to prove her wrong. I wanted her to see how much I loved him, and how much he loved me. If only she could see how we were meant to be together then everything would change. But for now, I had to settle with our secret visits at the pond.

The school parking lot was half full when I pulled in and parked in my usual spot. As I pulled my backpack out of the backseat, loud bass announced a vehicle had pulled up next to mine. I looked up to see who was making such a nuisance. Ivory Johnson hopped out of her car, but she wasn't alone. Leah was in the passenger seat. Leah flipped her hair back as she got out and they giggled their way into school, both completely ignoring me.

***

Leah and I had rearranged our schedules the previous years and switched some classes around to make sure we shared every class. We wanted to spend every precious moment of our senior year together. However, by fourth period it was evident that Leah had absolutely no intentions of speaking to me or making any sort of amends. She found the farthest possible seat away from me, and always made sure that she had someone else she could sit next to.

When the fourth period bell rang, I bolted out the door and headed to my locker to avoid Leah. She knew the affect she was having on me, as much as I tried to act like none of it mattered. Leah and I had been best friends for as long as I could remember. I didn't have any other friends. This was going to be a long year.

It dawned on me that I really had no one else. My stomach clenched in knots, my heart raced, and tears sprang into my eyes. Not wanting anyone to see me cry, I bolted to the girls' bathroom. The door opened right as I was about to walk in.

Leah paused for a moment in the doorway with her arms crossed, blocking me. Tears fell from my eyes and for once I didn't care. Leah smirked, and then waved her arm to allow me to enter, snickering as she walked away.

I ran into the only open stall available, sat down on the toilet, and attempted to dry my eyes, to no avail. A sob escaped my mouth and I covered it with both hands to try to stop any more noise. That's when I noticed the writing on the back of the door. There, in black permanent marker, someone I had once considered my best friend, had written "*Macy Reilly is a whore.*"

***

I spent the rest of my lunch hour trying to wipe off the writing before anyone else could see it. There was no way I could walk into the lunch room. Knowing Leah, more than likely she had Ivory, Mary Beth, and Wendy all waiting to see the show as well. I refused to give her and her friends the satisfaction. As I scrubbed the bathroom stall, I decided that this would be the last time I would ever let Leah Watson hurt me again. I should have listened to Jason. He knew exactly who she was from the moment they met. It was no wonder he didn't like her from the start.

When the fifth hour bell rang, I hurried into the main office to report that there was inappropriate writing on the bathroom stall that needed to be removed.

"Now, who would do such a terrible thing?" Ms. Lucy, our school secretary, asked.

I shrugged. "I have no idea."

"I'll notify the janitor right away."

At least I wouldn't have a daily reminder of Leah's backstabbing antics. I had more integrity than to rat her out, although it was tempting. But her day would come. I was certain of it.

***

By October, the stress was starting to weigh heavily on me. Besides school, homework, chores, and trying to secretly see Jason a few nights a week, I found that all I wanted to do was sleep. I rarely felt like eating, which I knew was attributed to stress and depression. I had lost some weight and my clothes were feeling baggier than normal.

Although my parents were fighting less, Mom was still not okay with the fact that Jason and I were together. She made rude comments when Dad was out of earshot, and I ignored her. She thought that the only time Jason and I were seeing each other was during chores on weekends.

My situation hadn't changed at school. Usually I skipped lunch and hung out in the library or I went to my car, just so I wouldn't have to watch Leah and her posse giggle, whisper, and twirl their hair. I didn't feed into it anymore, and I avoided it at all costs.

The only thing that mattered to me was being with Jason as much as possible. We had our weekend chores together. Brandon had become our chaperone. My parents found reasons for him to pop into the parlor or to help us with the milkings. When it got colder, we started meeting in Jason's truck, instead of at the pond.

"I'm sorry that being with me is causing you so much pain," Jason said as we snuggled under a blanket in his truck one night.

"It's not you that is causing the pain, it's everyone

around me."

"Yes, but it's because of me. If it weren't for me, none of this would be happening."

He had a point. "Well, you're worth it."

"Am I?" he asked. "Because I see what this is doing to you. It's wearing you down, Macy. You've lost weight. I see the bags under your eyes. You aren't happy. Being with me shouldn't be this hard."

We were silent for a long time. "Are you breaking up with me?" I finally asked. "Because that's what it sounds like."

Jason sighed. "I don't want to. Macy, I have never loved anyone like I have loved you. But look at what this is doing to you. It's tearing you up and I am the reason for it. I should let you go, but I don't know how."

"Well, what if I'm not ready for this to end?"

"Oh, I'm not either. I really thought your Mom would have come around by now. I should be taking you out on dates and showing you off. Instead, here we are, hiding, and each time we are out here I am afraid that your Mom will come knocking on my window at any moment."

"Pretty soon we won't even have this. Once the snow comes, I won't be able to go to the pond again until spring. Maybe we can meet after school, before Mom gets home from work?"

"I am still here working at that time. We will think of something. We will find a way. But in the meantime, I need to know that you are going to start eating and sleeping again. You need to take care of yourself."

"Jason, there is something I need to tell you," I said, looking straight into his eyes.

"Anything," he said.

"I'm worried that I haven't been feeling well for a different reason."

"What's wrong? Macy, are you sick or something?" I smiled briefly at his worried face.

"It's nothing like that. I think that I could be…pregnant." I studied him, gauging his reaction.

"Pregnant? Are you sure?" he asked, confused.

"Well, we weren't exactly careful. I can't be too sure, but I missed my period in September and now I can't even remember if I got it in August. I just realized it the other day. I need to take a test, but I don't know where I am going to get one without anyone seeing me. Are you mad?"

"Mad? How could I be mad?" He put his hand on my belly. "Do you really think we made a baby?"

"I don't know, but it's a good possibility. I was thinking that if I skipped out on chores this weekend, maybe I could get to Saint Cloud to pick up a pregnancy test. Since you will be here working, Mom won't think that I am sneaking off with you."

"Then that's one less day that we get to be together. Tell you what, how about I run to Sauk Centre tonight and pick one up? We can meet here tomorrow night and you can take it then."

"You want me to pee on a stick in front of you?" I asked, horrified. "I can't do that."

Jason kissed me. "Let's find out together if you are carrying my child."

"How did I get so lucky to have you in my life?"

"I'm the lucky one. Now get out of here. I have to go shopping."

***

Unfortunately, I couldn't meet Jason the next night. I knew he had purchased the test and that he would sit there and wait for me, but Mom invited Nana over for warm apple pie and ice cream. I didn't want to raise any red flags, and apple pie had always been my favorite. Even though I didn't have an appetite, I choked down the pie and then I went to lie down in my room, fighting the urge to vomit. I grabbed my backpack on the way up, crossing my fingers that no one would suspect a thing. As I tossed and turned in bed, I wondered if Jason and I really made a baby.

The next night Mom ignored me as I grabbed my empty journal and headed out to the pond. The air was crisp and cool, and I immediately started shivering in my sweatshirt. True to his word, Jason had parked in the trees, hidden from plain sight. The falling autumn leaves reminded me that winter was coming, and soon. Once the remaining leaves fell, it wouldn't be hard to spot his rusty old blue pickup from Chokecherry farm. He jumped out with a brown paper bag when he saw me approaching.

"What happened last night?" he panted.

"I couldn't get away. You bought it?" I asked, eying the bag.

Jason looked a little sheepish. "I didn't know which ones were the good ones, so I picked up a couple different kinds. You ready for this?"

"No," I said, grabbing the bag. "But it's now or never." I ripped the two boxes open and read the directions. I went behind Jason's truck and squatted, hoping that he wouldn't see me through the rearview mirror.

"Hurry up," he yelled.

"Shhh," I replied. Once I finished peeing on both sticks, I set the cap back on them and hopped in the truck. "It says to wait three minutes."

Jason stared at his watch as he gripped my hand

tightly. The next three minutes ticked by like an eternity.

"Okay, it's time," he said.

I took a deep breath. "Okay," I said, grabbing both sticks from the dashboard. I stared at them in disbelief.

"Well, what does it say?" Jason asked.

I handed them over to Jason. "Oh my God, Jason. We are having a baby. A baby! What are we gonna do?" I covered my face and started crying uncontrollably.

Jason pulled me into his arms. "Oh, Macy, it's okay. It's all going to be okay."

"What are we going to do now, Jason? What's going to happen when my Mom finds out?" For once, Jason didn't have an answer.

***

"Do you know the first date of your last period?" The doctor asked, making notes on her clipboard.

"Umm, not really. I think I got it in August sometime, maybe…I know that I did not get it at all in September or October." I wrung my hands together and stared at the floor.

"Were your periods regular before August?"

"Yes, they were," I answered.

"Have you taken a pregnancy test?" the doctor asked, making checkmarks on her chart.

"Yes, several of them. And they all came back positive."

"Okay," the doctor said. "Well, we will have you take another pregnancy test. Then we will try to squeeze in an ultrasound to see how far along you are. Once we know when you are due, we can discuss your options."

I swallowed the lump in my throat and took the

cup from her. "Thank you."

After the confirmed pregnancy test and quick ultrasound, we met back in her office. I sat across from her while she reviewed her notes. She dropped her file on her desk and looked over at me.

"It looks like you are about thirteen weeks along. So, you were right. You got pregnant in August. Looks like you are due May twentieth." I thought back to August. It must have been one of the first few times we made love.

"Okay," I said, not sure what to say next.

"Is there anyone you want to call? Your parents, perhaps?"

"No!" I said quickly. "They don't know...yet."

"I see," the doctor said. "Let's discuss some options here. We don't do abortions at the clinic here in Alexandria, but we can refer to you the Planned Parenthood in Saint Paul if you are interested. There is still time."

I shook my head firmly. "I'm not killing my baby."

"Have you thought about adoption?"

Again, I shook my head. The doctor nodded. "I see. If you ever want to discuss either of those two options, please let me know. We are not here to judge, we are here to be a support for you. I take it, since your parents don't know, you do not plan to see your family doctor for the duration of this pregnancy?"

I shrugged. "I guess I haven't thought about that."

"Okay. Well, let me get you some prenatal vitamins before you leave. The receptionist has your ultrasound pictures up front. Please read through all the brochures in your folder. Also, please make an appointment with our receptionist for your next visit. Prenatal care is very important, Macy. You will need to decide where you plan to deliver this baby. I see you live quite a ways away. You can't deliver around here."

"Thank you, Doctor." She shook my hand as I stood up to leave.

I stopped at the receptionist's desk to get my things and make another appointment. The doctor's questions were overwhelming. I never considered an abortion or adoption and I wasn't going to start now. When I got to my car, all I could think about was that when my Mother found out about this baby, it was going to change absolutely everything.

CHAPTER 16

MACY

By February I was barely functioning. Even though there was life growing inside of me, I couldn't find much happiness. I dreamed about it, my fairy tale life with Jason and our baby. But when I woke each morning, I had to remind myself that that life was still too far out of reach. There was too much at stake. Mom still didn't know, and I needed to keep it that way.

My belly grew into a perfect round circle. The only time I allowed myself to admire the changes in my body was when I was alone in the bathroom. I would rub my hands over my belly, and sometimes the baby would kick back at me.

My underwear dug into my skin and my jeans no longer buttoned. I used rubber bands to hold them together during school. I wore baggy sweatshirts no matter how hot I was. As soon as I got home, I changed into sweatpants, and I only took my sweatshirt off when I was alone in my room at night.

Jason found every opportunity to touch and talk to my belly. Our only time together was on Saturdays and

118

occasionally Sundays, and it was just during morning milking. Jason's hours had been cut down over the winter, but he was adamant that he still needed to milk at least once a day on the weekends to try to keep his hours up, and to see me.

For once, we were alone in the parlor. Brandon usually popped in and out during milking. Brandon missed seeing Jason during the week and he wanted to see him as much as I did. Brandon had spent the night at a friend's house, Dad was in Long Prairie for supplies, and it was Mom's Saturday to work at the bank.

Jason knelt on his hands and knees. He kissed my belly. "Can you hear me, little one? I'm your daddy." The baby was still. "I'm a little jealous of you. You get your momma all day and night, and I only get to see her on the weekends."

"Oh stop," I said, blushing a little. "This baby likes to kick and keep me up all night."

Jason stood to kiss me. I leaned in and wrapped my arms around his neck, kissing him hard. A few stolen kisses here and there were nice, but it wasn't the same. I missed being together like we used to. And as our kisses turned needier, I could feel how much he longed for me, too.

"God, I missed you," he said, as I unbuttoned his jeans and started sliding them down. "Wait a minute. Do you think it's safe? I mean, for the baby?" Jason pulled back.

I bit my lip to keep from laughing. "I think we will be just fine. Now get over here while there's still time."

Jason didn't need to be told twice.

***

"I've been thinking," Jason said a little while later.

"Oh, that's never a good sign," I shot back, grinning.

Jason grew more serious. "What is your plan once this baby comes? I mean, I think we need to discuss our future. This baby will be here before we know it."

"I know. This is all I seem to think about anymore. I just keep holding my breath each day, hoping that today won't be the day that Mom finds out. I figure that, if I can keep this hidden until I go into labor, then she won't have any choice but to accept this."

"I think we should move in together," Jason said. "I have been saving every penny, except for gas. I've got some money stashed away. We can find a place to rent and you can still go to college, and I will still be close enough to help out my grandparents."

"Oh, Jason, I would love that more than anything. But Mom will never go for it. It's bad enough that I am still in high school, pregnant and not married. There is no way that she will let me move in with you."

"So, let's get married then. You'll be eighteen soon, we can do it then. We can go to the court house and then there is nothing your Mom can do or say."

"Jason McNally, is that your idea of a marriage proposal?" I asked. I wasn't sure if I was excited or hurt. "I would hope that you wouldn't propose to me, in a milk parlor, with no ring, and the idea of walking into a court house, just so we can upset my Mother."

Jason held my hands. "You're right, I'm sorry. I didn't mean for it come out this way. I wish I could buy you the most expensive ring and give you the wedding you've always fantasized about—and not propose in a milk parlor," he said, looking around. "But our circumstances are different. I didn't plan for this and I know you didn't either. But we have a baby coming soon, and we need to figure this out, so we can be together, the three of us."

I nodded. "You're right, we need to make some plans."

Jason knelt on one knee. "Macy Reilly, I have loved you since the moment I laid eyes on you. You are beautiful and smart, and I can't live another moment without you. I know it won't always be easy, but I promise I will always try my best to make you happy and proud of me. I'm not rich, and I can't give you fancy things, but if you'll let me be your husband, I promise I will do my best every day to make you laugh. I can't give you the world, but I can give you all of me. I hope that that's enough. I don't have a ring, but I will. Will you marry me, Macy? Will you make me the happiest man in the world?"

"Yes, Jason, I will marry you," I answered, pulling him up for a kiss. "I don't need fancy things. I just need you, and our baby."

***

Jason and I were engaged! The winter was finally looking up. We had made some important decisions that I had been dreading. But Jason pushed, and thank God he did. We now had a plan, and I felt better than I had in months.

My birthday was still five months away. We could get married in June and move in together, right after the baby came. I still had time to apply to colleges and I could enroll for the fall semester. In time, I thought Mom would be okay with it all. We would be married by summer, and I would still get a college education. It may not be how she imagined, but this would be better. She would have a grandchild living close by that she could see any time she wanted.

After Jason left for the day, I decided to shower before laying down for a nap. No one was home yet, but I must have forgotten to latch the door. After I showered, I stood in front of the mirror in my bra and panties, admiring the side view of my baby bump.

Suddenly I heard a loud gasp. My Mother stood in the doorway, staring at my growing belly. Her eyes were huge, and her mouth was wide open in shock.

"Mom!" I yelled, using my shirt to try to cover my bulge.

"What the hell is this?" she said, coming into the bathroom. She grabbed my shirt and ripped it out of my hands. "You're pregnant?"

"Y-yes."

"Oh, my God. You're pregnant? Pregnant? No, this can't be." She ran her fingers through her hair. "This can't be happening. You and Jason have been having sex?"

"I've tried to tell you for awhile now, I just didn't know how. Yes, we are having a baby, in May." I grabbed a towel to cover myself.

"In May? Have you been to a doctor?" I have never seen her look so shocked and hurt.

My face flushed. "I have been going to Planned Parenthood in Alexandria." I couldn't look her in the eye.

"I knew you were gaining weight, but I didn't put two and two together. And you've been doing this all behind our backs. Oh, my God, Macy, how could you have let this happen? I told you that boy was trouble. I told you to stay away from him. And now, look at you, you're pregnant..."

I stood there silently, staring at the bathroom floor.

"No, no, this can't be happening. We need to take

care of this. We *will* take care of this." She turned to walk out the door.

"What do you mean when you say, 'take care of this'? There is nothing to take care of, Mom. We are having a baby," I said, following after her. I didn't care that I was still in my towel.

"Like hell you are," she screamed as she whirled around to face me. "You are not going to ruin your life over that low-life scum. We are taking care of this now."

"No, 'we' aren't taking care of anything," I said, squaring my shoulders. "This is my baby, and my life isn't ruined. You are just going to have to accept that."

Her eyes narrowed as she took a step towards me. I swallowed hard, forcing myself to not step back. "It's bad enough that I have a lying slut living in this house, but I refuse to let your life be destroyed in the process. You are seventeen. You have no idea what it takes to be a mother, or what it's like to live out in the real world on your own."

"I'm not on my own, Mom. Jason and I are going to get married and he will be there for me and our baby."

Mom swung hard and smacked me right across the cheek. It burned, and hot tears sprang into my eyes. I covered my cheek with my hand.

"Stop talking nonsense, Macy. This is not going to happen. It's over. This is all over. Now, get upstairs and put some damn clothes on."

I turned, ran upstairs, and threw myself on my bed. She slapped me. I had never seen her so furious. I could hear her on the phone, but I couldn't make out who she was talking to or what she was saying.

I didn't know what she was up to, but I knew it was bad. Jason and I were going to have to change our plans, and fast. I grabbed a suitcase out of my closet and started packing the few clothes that still fit me. I also grabbed my empty journal where I hid all my ultrasound pictures. As much as Jason didn't want to leave his grandparents, we really had no other choice. We were going to have to leave town. There was no way I could let my baby down.

I hid my suitcase in my closet when I was done packing. We would have to stop and pick up toiletries on the way. I was not willing to risk seeing her by going downstairs. Pacing my bedroom, I contemplated my next steps. As soon as Mom left, I would run downstairs and call Jason. We would have to leave tonight, before she did something that we would all regret.

Twenty minutes later I heard the door slam. Glancing out my window, I saw her heading to the pole shed, where Dad was working. The thought of her telling Dad and Nana made me nauseous, but now was not the time to be sick.

I ran downstairs and called Jason. His grandmother answered the phone.

"Hi, Mrs. McNally. Is Jason there?" I asked, watching the front door.

"Yes, dear. He is around here somewhere. Let me go find him," she said, laying down the receiver. It felt like an eternity before Jason came on the line.

"Jason, we have to leave tonight." I panted.

"Hold on, Macy. What's going on?"

"It's Mom. She walked in on me in the bathroom and now she – she knows." My voice cracked. "She hit me, and I don't know what she's going to do, but I know I can't stay to find out."

Jason was silent on the other end.

"Jason?"

"I'm here. What did she say?"

"She said that this wasn't going to happen, and that we aren't going to get married. I heard her on the phone, but I don't know who she was talking to. Now, she went out to the pole shed to tell Dad."

"This isn't good. Okay, we need to leave as soon as possible. Are you packed?" he asked.

"Yes, I'm all packed. I'll throw my suitcase out the window and I'll meet you where you park the truck."

"Ok, I'll be ready. What time should I be there?"

"I don't think I will be able to get out of the house until dark without anyone seeing me. So, after supper, if that will work?"

"Yes. Where should we go?" Jason asked.

"I haven't the slightest clue. Do you have any ideas?"

"How about we go to my parents' place in Texas? We can stay with them for a few days until we figure things out."

"It doesn't matter where we go, as long as I'm with you."

"Macy?"

"Yeah?"

"I love you."

"I love you, too." I hung up and took a few deep breaths. In just a few short hours, my life would be moving forward, not backwards. Once I left Chokecherry, I would never look back.

***

No one came around to help with the afternoon milking, nor did I expect anyone to. I didn't know what I was going to say when I came face to face with Dad, now that he knew. I couldn't imagine him reacting the way Mom did, however, I thought his disappointment would slice right through my heart. I didn't plan on getting pregnant, and I didn't plan on hurting anyone either. Once I left town, I knew I would be hurting everyone I loved. But I had to protect my baby from my Mom.

Leaving would hurt Dad the most. Maintaining the farm had become too much for him to bear alone, and he was pleased with how much they were keeping up with Jason being here. Now he was losing his full-time help, plus I wouldn't be there to do the milking. Brandon had his own chores and helped milk once in a while, but he would never be able to do all the milking twice a day during school. This would be a burden on them both, and I was not sure Mom would ever allow Dad to hire anyone ever again, now that she had proven her point.

Since I couldn't blow my cover, I couldn't say goodbye to anyone. The idea of writing letters to Brandon, Nana, and Dad crossed my mind, but I couldn't take the risk of Mom finding them before I left. She was probably ransacking my room at this very moment. As good as I had become at lying, this one was going to be the biggest lie yet, and I had to be extremely careful.

Now was not the time to start second guessing our decision. Mom needed time to cool off. Maybe she would come around by the time the baby came, and we could come back here and put our life back together. Jason wanted to stay close to his grandparents, and I wanted our baby to be around his or her grandparents as well. Maybe, just maybe, she could get past this.

I lingered in the parlor longer than necessary, just to avoid everyone. When there was nothing else left to do, I headed back to the house, hoping that supper would nearly be done, so I wouldn't have to face Mom alone. *Just a few more hours*, I repeated over and over in my head.

Taking a deep breath, I headed into the kitchen. The table was already set, and Nana was already sitting in her spot. Mother carried over a crock of stew to the table.

"Well, it's about time," Nana said as I came in. "What took you so long out there?"

I blushed. "Time just got away from me, I guess," I said, as I washed my hands in the kitchen sink. Mom refused to look at me, which suited me just fine. I sat down at the table when Dad and Brandon came in.

Nana knew right away that something was amiss, although she couldn't pinpoint why. After trying to start several conversations, she gave up and spent the rest of her meal in silence. I looked everywhere but at my parents. I knew, if I did, I would burst into tears.

As soon as dinner ended, Nana scooted out of there as fast as she could. Silently, Mother and I cleared the table and did the dishes. I felt as though I was holding my breath the entire time, just waiting for another fight, but none came. Once I had the last dish dried and put away, I hung up the dish towel and was about to retreat to my room when she stopped me.

"I forgot to pick up Nana's prescription earlier today. Will you ride with me to go and get it?" she asked.

I hesitated. She sounded so calm, which was a far cry from earlier today. If I said no, she would know that something was up. If I said yes, then that would leave Jason waiting in the bushes.

"Sure," I answered. Maybe she realized she over reacted. Maybe we wouldn't have to run away at all.

She waited for me as I put on my boots and jacket. Dad must have started the car, as it was already running when we went out there. As we turned onto Chokecherry Drive, we saw Jason coming down the road in his rusty blue Chevy pickup.

Oh shit. Mother slowed down just enough to get around him. His eyes widened in surprise when he realized I was in the passenger's seat. He raised his hand in a small wave. Mother couldn't wave back. She was gripping the steering wheel so tightly that her hands were turning white.

I started sweating in my jacket and had to unzip it to keep from passing out. I turned down the heat. Why wasn't Mom saying anything? As we rode in silence, I started to get a sinking feeling in the pit of my stomach.

"Were not going to Long Prairie to get Nana's prescription?" I asked after she turned on Highway 28.

"No, the pharmacy there is already closed. We have to get it in Sauk Centre."

"Oh," I said, not entirely believing her.

But when we got to Sauk Centre, she didn't pull in the parking lot. Instead, she went up to the stop light, and then turned on I-94 West.

"Wh-where are we going, Mom?" I asked, terrified.

She gripped the steering wheel even tighter. "To save your life."

I glanced up to study her face. Out of the corner of my eye I noticed something in the back seat. It was the very same suitcase that I had packed earlier today.

She *knew*. She knew about our plans to run away. And now, more than ever, she was determined to stop it. And I fell right into her trap.

CHAPTER 17

JASON

"Something's wrong, Jason. I can hear it in your voice. What's going on?"

I paused. "Mom, I have something to tell you."

Her voice shook. "Okay, honey. What is it?"

"We need to visit you guys for a little while." There, I said it.

"We, as in, you and Macy?"

"Yeah."

"We would love it! Why would you think otherwise?"

"Well that's the thing, Mom. She needs to get away from her mom. Her mom...hit her today."

There was an audible gasp on the phone. "Why on earth would she hit her own daughter?"

"Because she found out she's pregnant." I was met with silence. "Mom, are you there?"

"Y-yes, I'm here. She's pregnant? When is she due?"

"May twentieth. Her mom found out today, and she hit her. We need to get out of here as soon as possible."

"What about Grandpa and Grandma?" she asked.

"I'm sorry, but I can't worry about them right now. I need to get her out of there…before her mother does something stupid."

"I can't believe you're having a baby. And so soon! Yes, we will figure it out. You two better drive safe. You better call me when you stop for gas, even if it's the middle of the night. And don't worry about Grandpa and Grandma – we will find someone to do all their yard work."

"Thank you. I love you, Mom."

"I love you too, Jason. Do Grandma and Grandpa know?"

"I couldn't tell them yet. We couldn't tell anyone until Macy's parents knew."

"That makes sense. Put Grandma on the phone. I will tell her what's going on while you pack."

I handed the phone off to Grandma and headed to my room. I couldn't get to the bank to get my money out, but I thought I had enough cash to get us to Texas. Staying with my parents would help a great deal. It would give me time to find a job and save up for an apartment.

It took less than ten minutes to pack my belongings. Grandma was already in the kitchen, packing food for our journey.

"Need any help?" I asked.

She jumped. "I didn't hear you come in. No, I am packing you guys a couple of sandwiches. I think I have some cake that I can send, too. Oh, Jason. You're having a baby?" she whispered.

"Yes. We couldn't say anything until her parents knew. They found out today and based on her Mother's reaction…well let's just say it's best if we go away for a while." At the look on Grandma's face, I added. "Just until she cools down. Then we will move back here."

Grandma's face relaxed as she went back to making sandwiches. "When do you leave?"

I glanced at my watch. "I'll head over there right after dinner."

If I can wait that long.

***

The minutes slowly ticked by. All three of us sat at the table the rest of the afternoon, watching the clock. We tried making small talk, but we all had too much on our minds to hold much of a conversation.

When I finally couldn't take it any longer, I hugged my grandparents and thanked them for letting me stay there. Grandma choked back tears, and Grandpa's voice was husky.

"You are welcome back any time, Son," he said. "And Macy and the baby, too. All of you can stay here if you need. It's been a long time since we've had a little one around." He tucked a hundred-dollar bill in my coat pocket.

"I'll keep that in mind," I said as I headed to my truck.

As I turned on Chokecherry Drive, a sinking feeling formed in the pit of my stomach. We had spent months out at the pond or in the woods, hiding in my truck. Tonight, was no exception. But for some reason, something felt *off.*

As I neared the house, the sinking feeling deepened when I spotted Elaine's car turning from their driveway. *Oh, no.* There is no way I could turn into my hiding spot without her spotting me.

Having no choice but to drive past her, I held up my hand for a little wave. That's when I noticed that she wasn't alone. Macy was with her. What the hell was going on? I drove past the farm and kept driving down the road, in case Elaine was watching from her rearview mirror. I turned around after the Watson farm, contemplating my next move. Why was Macy with her? When were they coming back? What was I supposed to do now?

I drove around for an hour, and then I tucked my truck into the woods, waiting for Macy to arrive. I waited another hour, and then I drove past her house again. Elaine and Macy were still not back yet. My stomach sank. *Where did they go?*

Chapter 18

Macy

I stood there staring at him, unable to move. Jason still looked the same as he did twenty years ago. His hair had specks of gray in it, but his eyes remained the same ocean blue. I dreamt about those eyes for so many years, never believing I would ever see them again.

Jason cleared his throat. "I'm sorry to hear about Howard. He was a great man."

"Thank you," I said. "I didn't expect to see you here." I had hoped, but I had no right to expect it.

"I didn't know if I should come," he admitted. "But I wanted to see you. It's been a long time."

"Oh," I said, not knowing what else to say.

"You look good, Macy." He hadn't taken his eyes off mine.

I blushed. "Thank you, Jason. You don't look so bad yourself."

Brandon and Charlotte stepped out of the office with the owners and headed over to us. Jason hugged Charlotte and shook Brandon's hand. While he offered his condolences, I went back to packing up the flowers. I was suddenly extremely self-conscious in Jason's presence, and I needed to keep my hands busy.

Brandon and Charlotte grabbed a box and headed out to the car, leaving us alone once again.

"Can I help with anything?" Jason asked.

"I don't think so," I said, surveying the room. "I think this is pretty much it. We just have to drop it all off at the church."

Jason nodded. "How long are you in town?"

I shrugged. "A couple of more days, I suppose. I just have a few odds and ends to finish up before heading home."

"I see. Macy, do you think we could get together to talk before you leave?"

I shook my head. "I don't think that's a good idea."

"Please, Macy. I think it would do us both some good."

"Everything that happened was a long time ago, Jason. I think its best we leave it in the past. But I really appreciate you coming here tonight. It means a lot to me. Good night." With what little will power I had left, I walked past him and out the door, where Brandon and Charlotte were waiting.

Was this week my punishment for all the mistakes I made? Standing next my Dad's lifeless body for three hours while everyone paid their respects was more painful than I ever imagined. I played the 'perfect daughter' part well, but even I knew I was a coward. The shame of not being around these past few years was something I would live with forever. I never expected Leah to show up, much less try to make amends. And facing Jason for the first time in twenty years knocked all the wind out of my sails. As if all of this wasn't bad enough, I was heading back to Nana's cabin, to see if there was anything left of my marriage.

***

"You've been quiet since we left the funeral home. You okay?" Brandon asked after we left the church.

I sighed. "Yes. No. I don't even know anymore."

"Did you and Jason talk?" Charlotte asked.

"No. I guess there's not too much left to say after twenty years."

"Oh, I think there is," Brandon said quietly.

I mulled this over on the way to the farm. Perhaps Brandon was right. Maybe we did have unresolved feelings. Maybe, I shouldn't have been so quick to turn him down. But I knew I had to. I thought I had put all my feelings for Jason McNally behind me. But seeing him tonight, I wasn't so sure.

***

The cabin was dark when we pulled in. I tip-toed into the girls' room and gave them a gentle kiss. Ella stirred, but never woke. The bed in the main bedroom was only a full-size, so maneuvering in without interrupting Seth was impossible.

Seth turned and wrapped his arms around me, nuzzling my neck.

"I missed you," he said as he started kissing my neck and shoulder.

"Seth…" I warned.

He sighed. "I know we need to talk. But I already told you everything."

I turned to face him. "I need the truth, Seth. Do not lie to me. Are you two having an affair?"

"No, I swear. She came over one time to hang out with the girls."

"Yes, topless. I remember. What I need to know is why. You said it was to take the kids' minds off their

Grandpa, but I'm not entirely convinced."

"Why else would she have come over, Macy?"

"You tell me. I know something happened. You kissed her, didn't you?"

Seth froze. "Once," he finally admitted, trying to hold onto me tighter from under the sheets. "But I pushed her away and told her to stop. I told her I wasn't interested in cheating on my wife."

My heart sank. This was exactly what I feared since I saw that photo. Tears formed in my eyes.

"Where were my girls when this kiss happened?" I asked, trying to keep my composure. If I blew up now, I would never know the truth.

"Elvira had taken them in the house to get washed up from the pool. They didn't see a thing. I swear."

I exhaled. "Was she topless when she kissed you?"

Seth sat up in bed and ran his fingers through his dark hair. I sat up too, bracing myself for what he was about to say. He refused to look me in the eye.

"She said she wanted to take the girls swimming, to take their mind off everything. She came over, and yes, she asked me to put sunscreen on her back. Then she tied her top back on, and swam with the girls for a while. I didn't swim at all. I sat on the patio and got caught up on some files that I needed to sort through."

"After a while, Elvira came and said the girls needed to shower before dinner. So, I assumed Asia was going to leave. She had a towel around her and her bag, and I started leading her through the veranda. I thought she was following me. She called my name to stop me, and when I turned around, there she stood, topless."

"Asia just walked up to me and tried to kiss me. I pulled away from her and asked her what the hell she was doing. Asia said she thought that was what I wanted, too. I told her I didn't, that I was happily married, and I wasn't interested. She got pissed, and she left."

"Is that the end of it?" I asked through my tears.

Seth shook his head. "I wish it was. But she keeps texting me. I will show you all the messages, Macy. I have nothing to hide. At first, I was responding, telling her I had no interest in an affair. Finally, I stopped responding, and that's when it got worse."

"Worse?" I whispered, wishing I didn't know any of this.

"You know how we thought it was Augustus' photographer that leaked the picture to the tabloids?"

"Yeah," I answered.

"I think it was Asia."

"How so? Why would she want to implicate herself?"

"I think Asia hired a photographer to take those pictures. I think she sold those pictures to a tabloid because I turned her down, and she wanted to hurt me."

"What makes you think it was her?"

"Because she's been threatening me ever since. She's pissed that I turned her down, and now she wants me to pay."

"So, she's blackmailing you…" I asked?

Seth nodded. "She kept saying that once you saw the photos we would be divorced anyways, so we might as well see where this goes. Asia can't handle rejection. Since I refused to start this affair, she still wants to break us up and she wants to hurt my career. And this doesn't bother her at all. I am sure she made a ton of money selling those photos." He wiped his eyes. "But Macy, I swear to you, I would never do anything to hurt you. You mean too much to me."

I got up and tried to pace the floor. The bed took up most of the room, but I couldn't sit still.

"What did your partners say about all this?"

"They said we need to tread carefully. I showed them all the text messages. They are contacting her new lawyers and telling them we will go after them if she sells the photos. But…her lawyers could come back and say I sexually harassed her, and she is the victim in this whole situation. They are skeptical. Macy, this could ruin my career."

His words made my stomach clench. This was way worse than I predicted. Maybe an affair would have been better. I never liked Asia Prescott, and I could never figure out exactly what it was that bothered me so much. Now I knew. She was a manipulative monster and she only looked out for herself.

"This is awful. Why didn't you tell me this right away?"

"Because it all happened so fast and you were here with your Dad. You had enough going on, and I didn't want to add to it. I thought if my partners got a handle on this right away it would blow over by the time you got home. And now I just sit here and hold my breath, terrified that the next tabloid cover that comes out is going to be that picture."

"She sure knows what she is doing." I shook my head.

"She sure does. This came out of nowhere, and in a matter of a few days my life has been turned upside down. What if I don't have a job when I get back home? No one is going to want to hire me, not after this stunt. All I keep thinking is how would I be able to take care of you and the girls?"

I sighed. "Well, let's focus on one thing at a time. We can't change whatever is going to happen. Asia is going to do what she needs to do. And all we can do is sit on the sidelines and pick up the pieces when she is done. Let's just get through this funeral and deal with all this when we get back home, okay? I'm tired. Exhausted, actually."

I crawled into bed with my back to Seth. I couldn't look at him anymore. He got himself into this mess and now our whole livelihood hung in the balance. He didn't try to touch me again.

"I can't do this without you," he whispered.

"I know. Seth?"

"Yeah?"

"I am going to need to see those text messages."

When I finally drifted off to sleep, I didn't focus on Seth and Asia Prescott. Instead, my thoughts were only on Jason. Twenty years had passed since I saw him last, driving down the road on Chokecherry Drive. I wasn't emotionally prepared to see him tonight, or to see the sadness still lurking in those blue eyes.

***

The next morning, I got up early and found the oldest clothes I had. I decided to surprise Brandon and help him with morning chores so that we could all arrive at the funeral on time.

"Need some help?" I asked, walking into the parlor.

Brandon looked up, surprised. "I'll take all the help I can get."

I started milking, following Brandon's rhythm. Brandon ran things the exact same way my Father did, so it was easy to pick up where he left off.

"You don't look like you got much sleep," Brandon observed.

I shrugged. "Not really."

"Wanna talk about it?" he asked.

I shrugged again. "I wouldn't know where to start. I'm just so overwhelmed with, well, everything."

"Does this have anything to do with Jason?"

"Perhaps. Seeing him yesterday definitely rattled something in me. I just don't know exactly what that is."

Brandon was silent for awhile. "I think we all carry a lot of guilt about what happened."

"Why would you say that?" I asked, confused.

Brandon looked at me. "Macy, I owe you an apology of a lifetime. I want to tell you how sorry I am for everything that happened."

"Brandon, you're not making any sense. What could you be sorry for? You did nothing wrong."

"Yes, I did. Macy, I am the one who heard you on the phone with Jason, planning to run away. I didn't know why you were running away, but I was scared that I would never see you again. So, I…"

"So, you told Mom," I finished.

Brandon hung his head. "Yes. I have never seen her so upset. I heard her on the phone, calling churches for unwed mothers and then I put two and two together. If it hadn't been for me…"

"Brandon, don't say it." I inhaled deeply. "Thank you for telling me. I wondered for years how she knew, and now it makes sense. But you are not responsible for what happened. I am. I got pregnant and kept it a secret for as long as I could. I knew I wouldn't have been able to keep it a secret much longer. Had she not hit me, I don't know that I would have made that sudden decision to run away that day."

"But you never got to follow through, because of me."

"No, Brandon, it was because of her. I agreed to go

with her to the store, thinking she had calmed down and wanted to talk rationally. She would have found out about my plans anyways, she always did. Have you been carrying this guilt all this time?"

Brandon nodded and looked away. I leaned over and gave him a tight hug.

"Please don't carry this guilt, Brandon. I have carried this with me for twenty years. I can't have you feeling the same way."

"Well, it backfired. You never came back after that summer and I lost my sister anyways."

"Well, now you have me back, if you want me."

Brandon smiled. "It's been really nice having you around. I have needed you so many times over the years. Do you think you can ever forgive me?"

"There is nothing to forgive, Brandon. But I'm glad you told me. And I never thought I would say this, but I have enjoyed being here, too."

"You're enjoying milking cows?" Brandon teased.

I gave him a gentle shove. "I forgot how much they stink."

Brandon laughed. "Can I offer you some advice?"

"I'm all ears."

"I've kept in touch with Jason over the years. I think you should meet him and talk. He deserves that, and so do you."

***

Helping Brandon do chores refreshed my spirits. Knowing that Brandon told Mom about my plans to run away with Jason answered so many questions. It was written all over his face how much this had tormented him. But I would never hold him responsible. Not for any of this. I only wish we could have had this conversation sooner, just so he wouldn't have had to carry the weight of our Mother's betrayal on his shoulders, like I have.

All this animosity was ending today. No more dark family secrets and lies. No more staying silent. I got my brother back, and I was not messing up again. I couldn't change how things ended with my parents, and that was a regret I would carry with me forever. But it was a new future for Brandon and me, and our families. Somehow, I was certain that Dad had a hand in all of this. *Mission accomplished, Dad.*

I think Dad would have been pleased at how beautiful his funeral turned out. Sandy and Gracie came from the nursing home, as well as a few of the hospice team members. Although Leah did not attend, both of her parents came. Many neighbors, church members, friends and family came as well. Brandon, Charlotte, Seth and I sat in the front row, and our children sat in the second, giggling and whispering. The best part was that Brandon and I were there to comfort each other when we needed it.

Jason was in attendance too, although I didn't see him during the service. I could feel his presence, and I fought hard not to turn around and look for him. I didn't know what I was feeling, but I knew I wanted to see him again. I shouldn't have run away from him as fast as I did last night, but I completely froze up and didn't know what else to do.

After the service and burial, everyone started heading to the kitchen for lunch. The church ladies put together ham sandwiches, pickles, potato chips, and chocolate chip cookies. They also had coffee, water and milk. Seth and the girls headed to the kitchen, and since I didn't have much of an appetite, I stayed behind to start gathering up the flowers that seemed to have multiplied overnight.

A few minutes later I heard the door open and Jason walked in. I figured he would find me sooner or later, but as he walked up to me, my heart started to beat a little faster.

"Hi, Jason," I said, more confidently than I felt. "Thank you for coming." I leaned in and gave him a hug. God, did he smell good. He held on a little tighter than necessary, until I slowly pulled away.

"I needed to see you again. You look great, Macy." I blushed as he looked at me from head to toe, admiring my black dress.

"Thank you," I nervously tucked my hair behind my ears.

We stood there silently for a moment, until we both laughed.

"I'm sorry, I don't know why I am so nervous," I admitted.

"I am too. I am hoping that you will agree to meet with me."

I sighed. "Jason, I... I don't know how to answer that."

"I found him."

The hair stood up on my arms and the back of my neck. "Found who?" I asked, already knowing the answer, but needing to hear him say it anyway.

"Our son."

Chapter 19

Macy

"Where are you taking me?"

My Mother refused to answer. She looked straight ahead as she drove. Her lips moved a little, as if she were mumbling something to herself.

"Mom, why are you doing this to me?" My voice cracked.

"I'm doing the right thing. I'm doing this for you," she spoke so low that I almost didn't hear her. She was scaring me. "I have no other choice."

"Mom!" I yelled, trying to snap her out of it. "What is going on?"

She glanced my way briefly, and then looked back at the road. "One day you will thank me for this. You will. I'm doing the right thing."

I glanced around, looking for an escape. I put my hand on the door handle, contemplating jumping out. The speedometer hit seventy-five, and I knew that both my baby and I would die on impact if I tried to make the jump. I had to talk some sense into her.

I steadied my voice. "Mom, please talk to me about this. Where are you taking me?"

144

She took a moment to answer, and then she sighed. "I am taking you to Saint Patrick's Church in Fargo."

"Why would you take me to a church?"

She scoffed. "How about the fact that you completed an ultimate sin and you need to beg God to forgive you? You need some time with God, Macy. Hopefully He will forgive you, so you can change your filthy ways. I will not raise a dirty little whore in my house."

My face flushed as I stared out my window. "You think I am a dirty little whore, huh?"

"Yes, I do. No respectable woman would put herself in such a compromising situation. You ran around, having sex with that piece of shit, and look at what he did to you. I told you to stay away, and you wouldn't listen to me. Well, now it's up to me to fix what's broken, so that you will have some semblance of a normal life."

"And just how do you expect to fix what's broken? You think sending me to a prayer group will erase what happened? Yes, I've had sex, Mom. Praying about it won't take it away, and it is not going to make this pregnancy go away either."

"This isn't a prayer group, Macy. This church is a place for girls like you. Girls who got caught up with loser boyfriends and got themselves knocked up. Saint Patrick's is a church that is kind enough to let you stay there until the baby comes."

"Oh, I got it," I said. "This is a place for parents to hide their daughters because they are ashamed. You think that you can hide me away here forever? People will know I had a baby when I come home, Mom. After all, you're a little past your prime to be having children at your age, so everyone will know this baby is mine."

Mother shook her head. "Yes, this is a place to finish out your pregnancy. But your little bastard isn't coming home with you. He or she will be placed with a real mom and dad. This baby will go to a real family who will raise it in a loving home. Then you can go back to the life you always dreamed about. One day you will thank me for stopping you from making the biggest mistake of your life."

"My baby isn't a mistake. The biggest mistake I ever made was getting in this car with you." I leaned against the car door, hugging my belly, trying to stop my hands from shaking. I would never forgive her for this. Never.

***

It was late by the time we pulled into Saint Patrick's Catholic Church. Tall, heavy steel rods gated the church, and Mom had to punch in a code for the gates to open in the driveway. The gates closed as we pulled in, locking us in.

The church looked huge in the dark. A nun, who appeared to be in her sixties, waited for us on the bottom steps.

"You must be the Reilly's," she said, looking at my Mother. Mom nodded and then grabbed my suitcase out of the backseat.

"You must be tired from the travel, Mrs. Reilly," the nun said as we followed her inside.

"I'm fine," Mom answered. "This had to be done right away. Thank you for agreeing to see us so late tonight."

The nun nodded. "Of course. We will meet in my office and then Sister Mary Agnes will show Macy to her room." We walked up two flights of stairs and then down some long, dark hallways. This nun's office was the furthest down the hall. She waited for us to take a seat before she closed the heavy wooden door.

"Welcome. I am Sister Mary Eunice and I run this center for unwed mothers. We have a wonderful program here, and I am sure it will meet all of your expectations, Mrs. Reilly." I stared at the floor, not willing to look at either of them. She continued talking.

"Normally, we would give you both a tour of our facility, but since it is so late in the night, we will have to give Macy the tour tomorrow. Is that okay, Macy?" she asked, looking directly at me. I refused to answer.

"I would like to apologize for Macy's rudeness, Sister Mary Eunice. It appears my daughter forgot her manners, along with all common sense," Mom said.

Sister Mary Eunice waved a hand. "No apology necessary, Mrs. Reilly. Once Macy takes a few of our classes and signs up for job skills, we will see a noticeable difference in her behavior. I can assure you she will come home a better person, and stronger than ever. Now, let me buzz Sister Mary Agnes in, so she can show Macy to her room. Then we can finish completing the necessary paperwork." She shuffled some papers around from a folder on her desk.

I bit my tongue. I wanted to scream at them both and run out the door. But the gates were locked, and it was pointless to run. I had nowhere to go. Maybe, if I could get to a phone and call Jason, he could come and pick me up. I eyed the phone on her desk.

Sister Mary Agnes knocked on the door and peeked her head in. She didn't look much older than me. Sister Mary Eunice waved her in, and she stepped in and grabbed my suitcase.

"Please show Macy to her room," Sister Mary Eunice said.

The nun nodded. She looked at me. "Are you ready?" she asked. Careful not to acknowledge any of them, I stood up and followed her to the hallway, slamming the door behind me.

Sister Mary Agnes spoke in a soft, sweet voice. "Welcome, Macy. I'll show you to your room and where the restrooms are tonight, and then tomorrow, I will show you around the premises. I just started two weeks ago, so it will be good for me to see what I remember during our tour. Do you have any questions for me, dear?"

I shook my head, and then realized she couldn't see me in the dark hallways. "No," I said aloud instead.

"When are you due?" she asked.

"May twentieth."

"Oh, not too much left to go then. Well, right now, we have two other women here, and we just recently got a few calls for a few more. So, you will room alone for now, but if the other women do end up coming, you will mostly likely get a roommate." Walking through the church and to the adjacent building, we finally made it to my room.

"So, the restrooms are over here, and you will share it with all the women on this floor. You are in room 310, right in here," she unlocked the door and flipped on the dim light.

The room was tiny. Two twin beds butted up against each wall. There was one small end table in the middle, as there was not enough room for two. There were two small closets on each side, no more than two feet wide. Metal bars were welded to the small square window.

"Can I get you anything, Macy? A glass of water, perhaps?" I shook my head and sat down on the bed. I rubbed my legs and took a couple of shaky breaths, but that didn't help the gasps that started escaping.

"Oh, honey," Sister Mary Agnes came and sat down beside me. I leaned my head on her shoulders and started sobbing uncontrollably. "Shhh, it's okay. It's okay. It's all going to be okay, dear."

I shook my head. I tried to tell her through choked sobs, but no words would come out. I tried to tell her that after being here, my life would never be the same. My baby would not be okay. I would never be okay again.

***

For a small barricaded window, the light shone right through and the heat pressed against my face the next morning. My eyes were puffy and sore, and it took a few seconds to get my bearings. A sense of dread washed over me when I realized that this wasn't a nightmare after all. I really was living this horror.

I wanted to stay hidden, but my need to use the restroom forced me to do otherwise. I opened the door a crack, and seeing that no one was in the hallway, I made a dash for the bathroom.

When I came out of the bathroom, Sister Mary Eunice stood in the doorway to my room. She looked older in the light, and wore a stern face, much like my Mother did.

"I trust you slept well," she said. I wasn't sure if she was asking or commenting, so I didn't respond. She sized me up for a moment.

"You missed breakfast this morning. Breakfast is at 6 a.m. sharp."

"I didn't know th-"

"Don't be late again," she interrupted. "Your next meal will be at noon. Dinner is at 6 p.m. Now, please get dressed. We need to have you sign up for classes.

Go on, I'll wait." She stepped out of the doorway to my room, so I could enter. True to her word, she was still standing there a few minutes later when I emerged.

I stepped out in sweatpants and a sweatshirt. There wasn't much else in my bag that fit, and I wasn't going to squeeze into jeans that hardly fit anymore.

"Is that what your wardrobe consists of?"

"Pretty much," I answered.

"I see. Follow me," she said. I followed her down more long hallways and locked doors. We made it back to her office, and the same file folder that was on her desk last night was still there.

Saint Patrick's was bigger than I thought. They had a huge church with an attached boarding house for the nuns and pregnant girls. There was also a Catholic school and hospital, all on the same grounds, and all gated. My school records were in the process of being transferred over to Saint Patrick's. Once they received the class roster, Sister Mary Eunice explained that she would assign my classes accordingly, so that I would be able to graduate on time with the rest of my class. But there were some additional classes that were being added— sex education, abstinence, and pregnancy and health.

Sister Mary Eunice explained that every unwed mother was expected to help with all duties associated with keeping the place running smoothly. We were put on a rotating schedule. We rotated weekly between laundry, cleaning, meal preparations, and gardening. Five days a week we would be eating breakfast by 6 a.m., then school until noon. After lunch we would have classes until 2:30 p.m., and then we would start our assigned chores. Dinner was at 6 p.m., study/quiet time until 8 p.m., and then the lights go out. Saturday's would be spent cleaning the church from top to bottom. Although we were not allowed to attend church with the congregation on Sunday's, the priest would meet with us after for a small church service and confession time. Except for meal preparations, the rest of Sunday was spent in silence, prayer and reflection.

"How long do I have to stay here?" I asked, not caring about any of this.

"Usually, once the doctor clears you to be released, you can go home," she answered. "However, since you are due so close to the end of the school year, we will have to make sure you are up to date on all your studies so that you graduate on time."

"What's going to happen to my baby?"

Sister Mary Eunice sighed and closed my file. She folded her hands on the top of her desk and looked at me. "Macy, all of the children born here go on to wonderful homes. All homes are carefully vetted. Background checks are done to assure you that they are going to a perfect couple. I meet with the adoption agency often and help them pick the best families for these babies."

"I realize that this may be hard for you, at first. But, over time and a proper education, you will see that your baby deserves a beautiful life. A life that you can't possibly give them at your young age. Folks that come to us are desperate for a baby, so you know how much they will love them and care for them."

I shook my head adamantly. "It's my baby. No one will love this baby like I do. You can't take it away from me."

Sister Mary Eunice looked at me pitifully. "I'm sorry, Macy. It's already been done. You are a minor and your parents already signed the consent. I have three interviews in the next several weeks for potential parents. Listen, your parents love you, and they know what is best for you. Now, this is not the place to cause any sort of trouble. Don't make this harder on yourself than you need to, Macy. It never ends well."

***

Sister Mary Agnes gave me the tour of the premises after my meeting with Sister Mary Eunice. Sister Mary Agnes was a breath of fresh air compared to the old bat lady. Maybe it was because we were so close in age. Maybe it was because she was the first person who was nice to me. But mostly, she didn't judge me.

Since I couldn't attend classes until the school records came, I had to spend the rest of the morning in my room for "reflection" time, courtesy of the old bat. I laid in bed for two hours, hungry and desperate for a way out. There was no way I could climb those metal gates to get out. But if I could just get into Sister Mary Eunice's office, I could call Jason and he could come get me. He could cut some fence posts down by their garden and we could get away before anyone would notice.

By the time Sister Mary Agnes came back to get me for lunch, I had my plan in place. After everyone was asleep tonight, I would sneak over to the old bat lady's office and call Jason. I could be out of here before morning.

Sister Mary Eunice sat at the head of the large oak table. There were several nuns on either side of her. Two girls were already seated at the table. One looked like she was due last week, and the other barely showed a baby bump. I took a seat next to Sister Mary Agnes. She bowed her head, and when I looked around, I realized everyone else had their heads down too, so I did the same.

"Thank you, Lord for this bountiful food before

us. Please show us to always follow in your path. Lead us only to goodness. Forgive us as we are all sinners in need of guidance. In your name, Amen," Sister Mary Eunice prayed. Everyone in the room echoed "Amen", except for me. When I opened my eyes and looked at the table, I saw split pea soup, bread, and water.

I choked down the meal as best I could, knowing that whatever was coming for dinner could potentially be worse. No one spoke during the entire meal. In fact, no one even looked at each other. The only noise was the occasional clinking of the spoons, or slurping.

After dinner, I helped the nuns clear the table and wash the dishes, since the other two girls returned to their classes. Once classes ended, Sister Mary Agnes brought me over to the laundry to help the girls wash bedding and towels.

"Macy, this is Cassidy. Cassidy has been here for a little over a month. She is due any day now. And this is Whitney. Whitney has been here for almost three weeks now. She is due in June." I looked at both of them and smiled. They smiled back. "Do you want to introduce yourself?" Sister Mary Agnes asked.

"I'm Macy. I arrived last night. I am due in May, and my Mom made me come here," I blurted out.

Sister Mary Agnes patted my arm. "Well, ladies, I am going to head over to meal prep, and then I will be back to check on you girls," she said.

Once we were alone, Whitney spoke first. "My parents made me come here, too. They say my baby needs better than me."

"Well, it's probably true," Cassidy said. "Doesn't look like anyone of us could raise a baby."

"That might be true for you," I said curtly. "But I will do just fine raising my baby."

Cassidy raised her eyebrow. "You *will* do just fine?

Honey, you're here, just like the rest of us. Your baby ain't going home with you."

"The hell it won't," I said, more to myself than to her.

***

My head pressed against the door of my room, listening for any signs of life outside of it. I steadied my breathing, and when I was certain everyone had turned in for the night, I slipped off my shoes and snuck into the hallway.

I tiptoed down the hallway. My enormous belly slowed me down a little, but I was determined to get to Sister Mary Eunice's phone. I went down two flights of stairs, and then I peeked down her hallway to make sure no one was there. Not seeing anyone, I entered slowly, making sure the heavy wooden door didn't slam shut behind me.

As I crept up to her office door, I heard voices coming from inside. I pressed my ear to the door. There were two different voices, but they were muffled, and I couldn't make out who they were. The voices became louder as they got closer to the door.

Shit! I hurried over to the next door and rattled the door handle, but it was locked. Glancing around quickly, I saw the bathroom right across the hall. I ran over there and closed the door just as Sister Mary Eunice's door opened.

"Did you hear that?" Sister Mary Eunice asked.

"I didn't hear anything," the other woman answered. It sounded a lot like Sister Mary Agnes.

I leaned against the bathroom door, praying that they wouldn't come in and catch me. The nuns were quiet for a moment, until Sister Mary Eunice spoke.

"Well, I suppose we should retire for the evening.

But I think Cassidy is right. Macy Reilly is going to give us trouble until that baby comes. If you hear or see anything, you must report to me immediately."

"Yes, I will."

"Good night, Sister Mary Agnes."

"Goodnight."

I waited until I heard the door at the end of the hallway close. Gently I opened the bathroom door and peeked out. The coast was clear. I tiptoed over to her office and was pleasantly surprised that the door was unlocked. I felt around the wall until I found the light switch.

I eyed the phone as I made my way over to Sister Mary Eunice's desk. I was about to grab the receiver when a yellow file folder labeled "Reilly" on her desk caught my eye. This was the same folder that had been on her desk since I arrived. Hesitating for a brief second, I opened the folder.

There were admission forms, information on my due date and releases for the school district to obtain my school records. But the last page was a contract. I scanned the form until I got to the bottom. It read: 'A charity deposit of $10,000 will be made upon entrance of Saint Patrick's for the care and protection of the unwed mother. The other charity donation of $10,000 will be paid upon the release of the unwed mother.' Both Sister Mary Eunice and my Mother signed it, along with a check mark on the paid deposit line.

Where did Mom get this kind of money? Did Dad know about this? I had to get out of here, before it was too late. I closed the file and picked up the telephone receiver.

"What do you think you are doing?" Startled, I jumped back, dropping both the receiver and file folder. Sister Mary Eunice was standing in the doorway, her hands on her hips.

Chapter 20

Macy

The contents in the folder scattered all over the desk and the floor. I started gathering them up, avoiding eye contact. Sister Mary Eunice rushed over and ripped the folder from my hands. She scooped up the remaining forms that had fallen.

"What are you doing in my office at this hour?" she asked again.

My cheeks turned red while I tried to come up with an excuse. When nothing came to me, I just stood there, silently.

Sister Mary Eunice eyed me for a moment and then frowned. "I thought we had come to an understanding, Macy. I thought I had made myself clear about causing trouble. Good thing I turned around when I realized I forgot to lock up my office. It was quite a surprise finding you in here, going through my things."

"You mean *my* things. That folder has *my* name on it. My Mother is paying you $20,000 to keep me here for three months? Is that the going rate for taking

157

babies? Let me guess, you charge these adoptive parents the same? This place must be a gold mine."

"That's enough!" Sister Mary Eunice's voice echoed, and she slammed her fists on the table. I jumped. "I won't listen to your rumblings. Don't you dare accuse this church of doing anything other than saving these children from people like you. You don't deserve that child. That child deserves parents who are devoted to each other and to God. Having sex in a field with some hired hand and accidentally getting pregnant is not what your baby deserves. When are you going to see that your Mother is changing your future? She is changing that baby's future."

Instinctively, I place my hands on my belly. I glared back at her. "This is my baby. Mine. And Jason's. We have plans to be married and to raise this baby together. He isn't going anywhere, and neither am I. You are not taking this baby from me. I don't care what my Mom paid you."

Sister Mary Eunice smirked. "Well then, it looks like you have said your peace. And now I will say mine. Since it's apparent that you are not in the right state of mind, we need to look at other options to keep you safe. It's a good thing we are so close to a hospital with an entire floor devoted to mentally unstable patients."

"You wouldn't."

"Oh, but I would, dear. You see, we care so much about our unwed mother's health and their overall mental stability. I would hate to see the hospital use their straight-jackets, but sometimes patients leave them no other choice. Wouldn't that be a shame?"

I eyed her suspiciously, unable to tell if she was bluffing. "I don't want to go there," I admitted.

"No? If you don't want to head to the mental ward, then you will do as I say for as long as I say it.

Face it, Macy, there is no way out of here. All our gates are locked, and all of you are closely monitored. You may have snuck away once, but you will not get away with it again. From now on, you will have extra supervision. Sister Mary Agnes will be assigned to you for the duration of your pregnancy." She buzzed her from her desk.

"Oh, and one more thing before you go, Macy. Since you seem to have so much extra time on your hands, you will be assigned double duty for chores. Come in, Sister Mary Agnes, and thank you for rushing over at this late hour," she said as Sister Mary Agnes walked in.

"Is everything okay?" she asked, glancing at both of us.

"We are fine now. We just had a little misunderstanding. But from here on out, you will be assigned to Macy and making sure she follows all our rules. Should she step out of line, I am to be notified immediately. No phone calls, letters, or walks on the premises alone. And you will need to room with her until delivery. You are both dismissed."

***

The next two months ticked by slowly. Each day, hour and minute became excruciatingly painful. I missed home, even though I knew I would never look at my Mother the same way again. I missed Jason so much it hurt. The last time I saw him was when we passed him on the road. Where was he now? I couldn't imagine that my parents continued to let him work on the farm. Not after this. Was he thinking about me? Was he mad at me? Would he ever forgive me for getting in the car with my Mother?

I longed to hear his voice and to let him know that

I was okay. I missed everything about him. I missed his smell, his voice, and how tight he held me when we were alone, curled up in his truck, trying to stay warm. I even missed milking cows with him. We shared so many dreams and had such big plans for our future, all wrecked by my devious mother. I wouldn't blame Jason if he never wanted to speak to me again. I tried to push thoughts of Jason away during the day, so that no one else would see me cry. But each night I cried myself to sleep, and I could not have cared less if Sister Mary Agnes heard me or not.

Slowly I got used to life on Saint Patrick's, even though I was confined like an inmate. Sister Mary Agnes spent almost twenty-four hours a day with me, and the only time I was alone was when I went to the bathroom or showered. She slept in my room as well, although she never moved her belongings there. She dropped me off at classes each morning, and she was there when classes were done or when we took a break for lunch. She brought me to all my assigned duties, and she sat in my room reading while I studied at night.

She was sweet and endearing, and had we met in an alternative world, I could see us being friends. But I knew getting close to her would only bring me more pain. She had to report back to Sister Mary Eunice each day, so the less I told her, the better. She tried hard to get to know me, but when she pressed too hard, I shut down.

Sister Mary Agnes accompanied me anytime I was around the other girls. Cassidy had her baby long ago, and after she spent two days in the hospital, she was sent home. She did not get to say goodbye to any of us. Two new girls were staying at the convent. Kendall came not long after Cassidy, and she was due in July.

The newest member, Allison, came about a week later and she was due in August. Although I was not allowed to talk to any of them, I got the impression that they were not as comfortable being here as the Sister's made it seem.

The flowers were blooming all around the gates of the premises in early May. Sister Mary Agnes and I slowly toured the gardens one afternoon. Braxton Hick's contractions had started a few weeks prior, and today they were making me uncomfortable. As we got back to the convent, we were met by Sister Mary Eunice at the door. She had an envelope in her hand.

"This came for you," she said, handing me the already opened envelope, date stamped a few weeks prior. I took it from her and said nothing. I recognized my Mother's handwriting immediately.

By the time we got back to my room, I had to sit down from being so winded. Once I caught my breath, I took the letter out.

Macy,

This is not an easy letter to write, but I felt you should know. When I returned home, your Father and I sat down with Nana to explain all the indecencies that have been happening around here. She was devastated by your actions and all that have transpired since. She felt like this was all her fault as she knew about the two of you and kept it a secret from us.

The stress took such a toll on her, and two weeks ago she had a heart attack. Dad rushed her to the hospital, but there was nothing they could do. Nana passed away with a broken heart.

Her funeral was last week. She would have wanted you to be there, Macy. I am sure she is even more disappointed that you couldn't be there with the condition that you are in. Hopefully one day she will be able to forgive you, too.

Life here has not slowed down, now that your Father and Brandon have been left to take care of the farm. We trust that upon your return you will be willing to work hard to make up for all that has been lost. This whole situation has really taken a toll on us all.

Sister Mary Eunice has informed me that all your grades are up to speed for graduation. I have decided to help you out by applying for colleges on your behalf. You have been accepted to several colleges in Saint Cloud, and we are still waiting for a few others. We will discuss which

one you will be attending once you
return home.

Take care,
Mom

The letter slipped from my fingers and fell to the floor. I covered my face with my hands and fell back on the bed.

Sister Mary Agnes rushed over to me and knelt on the floor. "What's wrong, Macy?"

"My...my Nana died," I blurted through my tears. "She had a heart attack, because...because of me."

Sister Mary Agnes hugged me for a long time while I cried. She picked up the letter and read it. When my sobs subsided, she rubbed my arm and spoke quietly. "Macy, this letter is appalling. Your Nana didn't pass away because of you. She passed away because God was ready to call her home. The fact that your Mother is trying to further hurt you because you got pregnant is totally unfair and unjustified. I don't mean to sound harsh, but quite frankly, this pisses me off."

I wiped away my tears. "You don't think she died because of me?"

"Absolutely not. I don't know your mom, but based on this letter, I surely question her character. You didn't want to come here, did you?" I shook my head. "I see. So, tell me what led you here in the first place."

I paused for a moment. Even if she ratted me out, it wouldn't change the outcome, so I told her about Jason and how everyone loved him, except my mother. I explained that we fell in love and had plans to get married and raise our baby together. How Mom slapped me when she found out I was pregnant, told me I was a slut, and how she tricked me into driving here. Finally, I told her how she was paying this church $20,000 to take my baby away from me.

Sister Mary Agnes listened intently the whole time, a grave expression on her face. It felt so good to let all of this out and tell someone about my mother's deception. By the look on her face, I knew she had no clue that this church was charging "donations" for adopting out children against their mother's will.

Her lips were pressed in a thin line when I finished. "I see," was all she said.

Did I shoot myself in the foot by telling her all this? It didn't matter either way, I decided. What more could possibly come of this horrible situation?

***

Pain shot through my lower back as I tried to turn over in my sleep. No matter which way I turned, I couldn't get comfortable. After tossing and turning, I finally managed to crawl out of bed to go to the bathroom.

As I stood up, I could feel something wet dripping down my leg. *I'm pissing my pants*, I thought as I tried to hurry to the bathroom. I made it to the hallway before I gasped out loud and bent over, trying to get the pain to subside. Braxton Hicks had nothing on the pain roaring through my body.

I knelt and crawled over to the wall. Bracing my back against the wall helped with the lower back pain, but my stomach was cramping. I moaned and held on to my body tight. The floor was wet all around me. I took some deep breaths, waiting for the pain to ease.

Sister Mary Agnes came flying through the door. She slipped on the wet floor as she headed to the bathroom. She caught her balance and pushed the door open.

"Macy? Macy, are you in here?" she panicked. I

tried to call out, but another round of cramps stopped me. "Macy!" she shouted as she spotted me on the wet floor.

"Oh, honey, you're in labor! We need to get you over to the hospital!" She grabbed my arm and pushed me up. We both struggled.

"The mess…" I panted.

"Oh, don't worry, Macy. We will take care of that. We just need to get you to the bottom of the stairs. There is a wheelchair down there and I can push you over to the hospital." I grunted and panted down flights of stairs, gripping her for support. Sister Mary Agnes grabbed the wheelchair from a closet, and I collapsed into it.

She rushed us over to the hospital in record time. Nurses scurried around until she was able to flag one of them down to ask for assistance.

"Is she from the convent?" the nurse asked. Sister Mary Agnes nodded. "Ok, she needs to deliver upstairs then. We will call Sister Mary Eunice over for the admission forms."

By the time I got admitted, my contractions were coming every couple of minutes apart. The pain ripped through my body and I threw up twice. Sister Mary Agnes pulled my hair back and held my puke bag, patting my sweaty head with a cold wash cloth.

Sister Mary Eunice came a few minutes later with a clipboard and thrust it in front of my face. She held out a pen.

"Macy, we need you to sign these admission papers for the hospital. This has to be done before the doctor will deliver."

I glanced at the first form. It said 'Admission to Saint Patrick's Hospital' on the top. After my contraction passed, I signed the form. The next one was a billing form. I signed that one as well. I handed the clipboard back as another contraction came. She glanced through the paperwork.

"You forgot one. Sign here," she said, holding the clipboard. After I signed it, she looked at the nurse. "She's ready to go. Sister Mary Agnes, please see to it that Macy is well taken care of." She peered down at me and patted my hand. She put on a fake smile and kind voice. "Macy, this is almost over. Soon you will get to go back home, and all will be forgiven. You take care now."

Chapter 21

Jason

Three months. It had been three long months since Macy and our baby disappeared. The agony only got worse with each passing day. I was no closer to finding out the truth than the day they drove away. Where did they go?

I let them both down. I should have gotten there earlier. I should have barged in the door and taken her as soon as she called me. I should have called the police and had Elaine arrested for slapping her. My biggest regret was waiting until dark. Who knew what happened at their house from the time she called until I last saw her driving away? Why didn't I go right away?

The sleepless nights were wearing on everyone around me. I became increasingly short, moody and downright explosive. The first few weeks, my Mother called non-stop, wanting to know if there was any news. Eventually I stopped taking her calls, and I could hear my grandparents whispering on the phone, which only angered me further.

The clanging of wrenches in Grandpa's garage did not keep my mind off Macy, as I had hoped. I spent hours out there just to avoid the questions and lingering looks. But my awful conversation with Elaine and Howard continued to play over and over in my mind.

"I'm not leaving until I know where she is," I said defiantly when I showed up unannounced one afternoon. "You can't keep her from me."

Elaine laughed. "You are such a stupid young boy, aren't you?"

I felt my hand ball into a fist. For the first time in my life, I wanted to hit a woman. I wanted to hit *her*. "Where is she?"

Elaine put her hands on her hips, and her eyes narrowed. "This is your last warning, McNally. Show up on my property again, and you will have an Order for Protection on your ass so fast you won't know what hit you. You are not welcome here. You need to leave us the hell alone."

My voice softened when I noticed Brandon was watching from the window. "I'm sorry, Mrs. Reilly. I have a right to know where she went. It's my baby, too."

"It's unfortunate, then, that Macy was so terrified of you that she couldn't tell you how she really felt."

"What are you talking about?" I demanded. "She wasn't scared of me."

"Oh, but she was. She cried and cried and told us that she was scared to tell you what she really wanted. We had no choice but to protect our daughter and her wishes."

I crossed my arms. "Her wishes?"

"She didn't want to raise a baby with someone like you. She was devastated to learn she was pregnant. She wanted to give the baby up for adoption but knew you would never allow it. She asked us to help her— and we did."

My voice cracked as I shook my head. "She was afraid of you, not me. She wanted our family. Why are you lying? Please, just tell me where she is."

"You're wasting your pathetic breath. I will never tell you where she is. She doesn't want you to know. She doesn't want anything to do with you," Elaine scoffed.

"Please, Mrs. Reilly," I choked out, blinking away tears. "Please."

"That's enough," Howard said softly as he approached me from behind. Elaine went into the house, without saying another word.

"Mr. Reilly, where did she take her?" I asked, turning toward him.

He sized me up for a moment, and then he exhaled. He patted my shoulder. "Damn it, Jason. I wish it didn't have to come to this."

"Me either. I just need to know she's okay. And that my baby is okay."

"They are both going to be okay, Jason. That's all I can tell you. But Mrs. Reilly won't hesitate to file an Order for Protection if you show up again. It's time to stop all this nonsense. No more calling and no more showing up here."

I wiped a tear from my eye and turned away, heading towards the truck. "I'll never fucking stop. Never." I revved up the engine and peeled out the driveway. When I glanced in the rearview mirror, I saw Mr. Reilly's shoulders sag as he watched me drive away.

That was three months ago, and I didn't even know if my baby had been born yet, or if it was a boy or a girl. I didn't know if they were safe, or what happened to either of them. But I did know that Elaine was lying about everything she said. Macy loved me and wanted us to be together. And she would never have wanted to give our baby away.

Each day that passed without Macy was another day I let her down. If I knew where she was, I would have gone to get her. *Would she ever forgive me for not being able to help her?* I grew more desperate by the day. *Please, God, help me find them. Just give me a sign. She needs me.*

I waited for an answer, or an epiphany, or some sort of sign. When none came, I punched a hole in the garage wall. My hand started swelling as I headed to the house, but I didn't care. The pain wasn't any worse than what I had been feeling for almost three months.

Where the hell are they?

CHAPTER 22
MACY

I never understood what people meant when they said that the best day of their life was also the worst day of their life. Well, I never understood that until that day. After two hours of pushing, I gave birth to the most beautiful baby boy that I had ever laid eyes on. My son, born on May 15th, 1994, came in weighing 8 pounds, 4 ounces. He was absolutely perfect.

The doctor placed my crying boy on my chest. I held him close as he slowly started to get his color. A wave of joy and love rushed through my body, even down to my toes. A real, instinctive, maternal love. A love I never knew was possible, until then.

Sister Mary Agnes clapped her hands together and grinned broadly. "Oh, he's beautiful Macy! Look at him!" She pulled a chair up to get a better look. "He looks just like you."

I shook my head. "No, he looks just like Jason. He has his oval face and crooked nose. He even has his long fingers," I said, running my fingers over his.

"What are you going to name him?" Sister Mary Agnes asked after a while.

I frowned. "I don't get to name him. His new parents will get to pick out a name for him. And I'll never know what it is."

"That might be true. But I think he should get a name from you. You're his Mother, too."

I thought about it for a moment. "Jason and I threw some names around once or twice, but with all we had going on, we never got to formally pick one. Let's see…he really liked Sawyer. So, I guess I will name him Sawyer. Yes, Sawyer Howard McNally."

"He looks like a Sawyer. I love it. You did real good, Macy. I'm proud of you."

The nurses finished cleaning everything up. "We need to go wash the baby now," one of them said.

My heart started tightening in my chest, making it hard to breathe. I only had a few precious minutes with him. I wasn't ready to let him go. Not yet.

"Is he coming back?" I asked. The nurse never answered me as she held her arms out to take him. I gripped on to him harder, trying to hold on to him a little longer. Tears blurred my vision and I started kissing the top of his forehead, hair and fingers. The nurse hesitated, and then she took him right out of my arms and walked out the door.

I tried to sit up on the bed, but Sister Mary Agnes grabbed my arms. "Whoa, there. Sit back down, Macy. You are in no condition to be walking around this soon. Your stitches could tear."

Bile rose in the back of my throat and hot tears hit my cheeks. "They're not going to bring him back, are they? They're not going to let me see him again." Suddenly it hit me. What if I never saw him again? I couldn't let him go. Not yet. Not ever.

"You will see him again, Macy. I'll make sure of it."

***

The hospital room conditions were much more pleasant than the rooms at the convent. Even though the unwed mothers had to deliver on a different floor, the rooms were much larger, and the windows weren't barricaded shut with metal wires. For the first time in almost three months, I was able to watch TV.

However, none of the upgrades made me feel better, not even the food. Sister Mary Agnes left so I could get some rest. The nurses checked on me often enough, I suppose the old bat lady didn't think I needed another babysitter.

The Tylenol didn't do much for my physical pain. The pain of not being with my baby overshadowed any physical pain I could have felt. This was pure torture. He was in some other room, alone, in this hospital. He should have been with me, on my chest, our hearts beating together in unison. I ached for him in a way that I never ached for anyone or anything else in my life. It hurt like hell.

Throughout the day and into the evening, my emotions ranged from rage towards my Mother for doing this to me, to being lonesome for Jason, and the sharp, throbbing ache of the physical need to hold and smell Sawyer. I wept constantly.

The nurses popped in occasionally. They refilled my water, helped me to the bathroom and they fluffed my pillows. They checked my blood pressure and made notes. Each time one of them came in, I asked when I was going to see my baby again, and each time they would answer with "I'll have to get back to you on that." That same nurse wouldn't return.

A gentle knock woke me from a light sleep. None of the nurses ever knocked, they just walked right in. I stared at the door. Sister Mary Agnes peeked her head in, with a big smile on her face.

"Care for some company?"

I shrugged and looked at the clock. It was almost midnight. Sister Mary Agnes came in and shut the door firmly behind her. When she turned around, she was carrying Sawyer.

I gasped and hit the button on my bed to make my bed sit up. "They are letting me see him?"

Sister Mary Agnes quietly placed him in my arms. She opened the folding chair in the corner and set it up closer to my bed. She set her bag down and sat beside us.

"I told you I would make sure you saw him again."

I grinned. "How did you make this happen?"

Sister Mary Agnes grew serious. "Macy, this isn't going to be a long visit. There is only one nurse on this floor because you are the only one here. They couldn't pull any of the nurses off the birthing floor, and your nurse needed to go on lunch break. I just happened to be loitering around, and I casually offered to help watch Sawyer while she took her lunch. She will be back in about a half hour. So, I am giving you about twenty minutes."

I was awestruck. "Thank you. Thank you for letting me see him. It means more to me than you will ever know."

She waved her hand. "No need to thank me. Sawyer needs this just as much as you."

Sawyer was alert and wide awake. With the dim lamp on in the corner, it was hard to see what color his eyes were. He had a bath since I had seen him last, and he smelled fresh and clean. His head was covered with little black hair. He chewed on his fist as he looked at me.

He could feel me. He could feel my heart beat and

when he looked at me, I knew he knew that I was his Mom. Love filled my heart all over again. I opened his blanket and rubbed my fingers over his tiny fingers and toes, and I kissed them over and over. I rubbed my hands down his cheeks and watched how he responded by slowly closing his eyes.

Sister Mary Agnes silently watched the clock and us. I knew our time was winding down, and I had to mentally prepare myself to let him go again. The Sister reached in her bag and pulled out a Polaroid camera.

"Okay, Macy, this stays between us. I am going to take two pictures and hope no one notices that any are missing. I will take one of just Sawyer, and one of the two of you. How does that sound?"

I swallowed a lump and nodded. "That would be perfect," I whispered. I smiled broadly while she snapped the picture of the both of us. Sawyer's eyes were wide open. She got really close to his face to capture all his features and took the other.

"I'm sorry, Macy. But I need to get him back in the nursery before that nurse catches us."

"I know," I replied. I was losing him all over again. I blinked back tears and looked down at his beautiful face. "I'm so sorry, Sawyer. Please know that this is the hardest thing I will ever have to do. I love you so much. Daddy loves you so much, too. I'm sorry he couldn't be here. I hope you have a wonderful life, even if it's without us. It shouldn't have to be this way. I have never loved anyone like I love you and I never will." I kissed his chubby cheeks. "Please forgive me," I whispered. With all the strength I could muster, I handed him back to Sister Mary Agnes.

Sister Mary Ages blinked away her tears. "I'll be back to check on you once the nurse gets back."

Once again, I watched my son leave the room,

knowing that this is the last time I would ever see him again.

***

True to her word, a relieved looking Sister Mary Agnes came back after the coast was clear. Doing this put her in a difficult position, but I couldn't feel guilty about it. I got to see, hold, and smell my son for twenty minutes. Nothing in my life had ever felt so right.

"Did the nurse suspect anything?"

She shook her head. "I don't think so. When she came back, I was rocking him in the rocking chair. He fell asleep and didn't stir when I laid him back in his crib. I told the nurse I needed to check on you before I turned in for the evening."

I chose my next words carefully. "Sister Mary Agnes, I just want to say thank you again for doing this for me. I don't think any of the nurses have any intention of letting me see him again."

Sister Mary Agnes grabbed my hand tightly. "Macy, they were given direct orders to not let you see the baby. I know that's hard to hear, but they are just doing their jobs. Sister Mary Eunice says that it's best this way. She says that it is far easier on the birth mother, and that the baby won't be as confused. Then the baby can bond with their new family right away."

"Do you think that's true?"

She shook her head. "If I did, I wouldn't have snuck him in here tonight. Remember, this stays between us. Where did you put the pictures?"

I pointed at my suitcase. "There is a little rip in the lining. They are carefully hidden. I don't plan to take them out until I get home. Well, I doubt they would even be safe in the same house as my Mother. I'll have to find the perfect hiding spot."

"Good. Well, I need to turn in before Sister Mary Eunice comes looking for me. Are you going to be okay?"

"No...No, I won't. I will never be okay again."

Sister Mary Agnes patted my hands. "There's got to be a better way. There has to be something else I can do."

"You've already done more than I ever could have asked."

"And yet it's not enough, is it?"

***

I was just finishing breakfast the next morning when Sister Mary Eunice finally made her appearance. She made my skin crawl. Being in the hospital was such a nice break from her, but I knew it wouldn't last forever. She still found ways to torment me.

"Good morning, Macy. How are you feeling this morning?"

"How do you think I feel? Do you see me holding my son right now?"

She let the comment slide as she gazed out the window.

"I spoke with Elaine this morning to let her know that the baby came yesterday. She asked when she could expect you to return home." She paused.

"Did you tell her I wouldn't be returning home? Since my son is not welcome there, I won't be returning there." I crossed my arms.

Sister Mary Eunice's eyes widened as if she were surprised at my statements. "Oh, dear. Are you still under that assumption? Whatever would make you think that?"

"I told you I wasn't leaving here without him. You can't take him away."

Sister Mary Eunice walked over to me, and bent her head down, close to my face. She had an amused expression on her face. "I'm afraid it's already done. I called his new parents while you were in labor. They rushed down here to see him. The doctor did a thorough health exam. The doctor saw no reason for him to have to stay here any longer. He is at his home now, with his Mother and Father. I'm surprised no one thought to tell you this."

Anger flooded through me as I clenched my hands together, digging my nails into my skin. That lying bitch! I wanted to smack that smug smile off her face. I wanted to scream at her and call her out on her lies. I wanted to tell her that I knew my son was still here, because I got to hold him and love him.

Reluctantly, I said nothing. The repercussions of challenging her would only hurt Sister Mary Agnes. I had to keep my word and stay silent about last night, even if it killed me.

"This is illegal, and you know it. You won't get away with this."

"I won't get away with what, exactly? No one made you sign those adoption forms. You signed them of your own free will."

"Adoption forms?" Then it dawned on me. Those weren't admission forms for the hospital. Those were forms terminating my parental rights for my son.

***

Sister Mary Eunice's words echoed in my head. Why did she feel the need to lie to me? More importantly, why was she trying so hard to make me suffer even more? I should have been suspicious when she asked me to sign those forms. I should have known better. Even nuns couldn't be trusted.

Sister Mary Agnes was another story. As much as I resisted letting her know anything about me, I am so thankful that I confided in her. Even though I knew she would report back to the old bat lady, I found myself in a delicate position of not having anyone close to me around. In my weakest moments, she was there for me. She held me when I cried, and she blinked away tears after hearing my story. I would consider her my closest friend. Possibly the only friend I had left. Had I not shared my story with her, she may not have snuck my baby in to see me. And for that, I was immensely grateful, and I always would be.

I had made some big mistakes being with Jason. I hurt a lot of people. Maybe my Mother and Sister Mary Eunice were right. There were consequences for all my actions. I'd lost everyone I ever loved. Leah, Jason, Nana, and now Sawyer. Losing Sawyer hurt the most. I'd committed the ultimate sins, and now I would pay the price the rest of my life. I would never be able to forgive my Mother for putting me here. But I also knew there was no one else to blame but myself.

I spent the rest of the day in isolation. The nurses barely checked on me. They refused to make eye contact, and they wouldn't answer my questions. "The Doctor will be in later," was their only response. Even though the amenities were nice, I missed Sister Mary Agnes' company. When she was a no show at 10 p.m., I figured I had been deserted. She had risked it all by stopping over last night, and to stop again could raise eyebrows with the nurses.

A rough shaking woke me up a few hours later. The room was pitch black. Startled, I opened my eyes and jumped when I saw a dark figure standing over me.

"What the hell?" I shouted.

"Shhh. Macy, it's me." It was Sister Mary Agnes.

"What are you doing? You scared the shit out of me."

She giggled. "I didn't mean to. Get dressed. It's time to get you guys out of here." She fumbled around in my suit case.

"What do you mean?"

"I will show you how to get out of here unnoticed. I will take you to the emergency room parking lot, where the fence stays open. After that you are on your own. You need to do this now, while it's still dark outside. There is a gas station about three miles away. If you can get to it, you can call someone for help."

Even though the room was still dark, I realized she had Sawyer tucked in her arms. I sprang out of bed and threw on a pair of sweatpants and a sweatshirt. I threw my hospital gown on the bed and turned to face her. She pushed a small, black backpack towards me.

"Put this on. There are a couple of bottles, diapers and an outfit in here for him. But it won't last long. You are going to need to get to a store, and fast. There is some cash in the inside pocket to get you what you need until you get home."

"Are you sure about this? You won't get in trouble?"

"No one knows I'm here. I'm supposed to be sleeping. But there is a couple coming to pick him up in the morning. If you don't do this now…"

"I know, I know. How can I ever thank you?"

Sister Mary Agnes handed me Sawyer and hugged me at the same time. "Knowing that you are all together is all I need. I will pray for you, Sawyer, and Jason. Be happy, Macy. You deserve it. Now scoot before I chicken out."

She slowly opened the door and peered out into the darkened hallway. It didn't look like anyone was at the nurse's desk, so she opened it a little wider. I followed as she took a right, opposite of the nursery and nurse's station, and headed to a stairwell. My vagina burned with each step, but I couldn't slow down. Not when I was this close to getting us out.

At the bottom of the stairwell, she turned to me. "Ok, right outside of this door is a door that leads to the parking lot. There is no fence at the end of the lot. Follow along the trees so you are not seen under the lights. Got it?"

I nodded. My heart pounded in my ears as sweat rolled off my forehead. She opened the door, and making sure the coast was clear, she turned to me and mouthed. "Go!"

I followed her instructions carefully. Sawyer nestled into his blankets, sleeping soundly, even with my sudden movements and my heavy panting. Even with the evening breeze, sweat beads dribbled off my temple. With a backpack on, and eight-pound baby, and a sore bottom, I wasn't moving as fast I needed to. As I dodged from tree to tree, I inched closer and closer to the end of the parking lot.

A wave of relief rushed through me as I crossed the road, away from the fence. Less than a half hour ago, I thought my life was over. I thought I would never see my son again. And now here we were, on our way to total and utter freedom. We did it. We escaped. We were free.

Adrenalin pumped through me as I walked. Sister Mary Agnes said the gas station was only three miles up the road. We would be there in about an hour or so, depending on if Sawyer needed any breaks. I just needed to push through the physical pain and remind myself to take it easy.

Ten minutes later, I heard sirens go off at Saint

Patrick's. I turned back around to see the yard lights flashing and the emergency parking lot fence automatically close. Lights were turning on all over in the hospital rooms and even some in the convent. They must have realized we were gone.

Glancing around, I noticed there weren't too many places to hide. My chest tightened when I realized the fields surrounding the area were all open, and the trees were sporadic. Maybe the ditches would be deep enough for us to crouch down in. We would either have to hide down there, or I was going to have to walk across some fields to search for better hiding places.

Headlights flashed ahead of us. They couldn't be from the convent as it was in the opposite direction, but we waddled down into the ditch and sat down until the car passed. Just as I tried getting up again, another set of headlights came from the direction of the convent. I held my breath, crossing my fingers that no one would stop.

When the coast was clear, we crawled back up the ditch, but I didn't go back on the road. We would waste too much time having to hide every time a car passed. My lower back and arms were getting sore and my vagina rubbed against my pad, making it burn. I could feel the blood clots leaving my body as I walked. We had no choice but to walk across the fields for better hiding, until we got to the gas station.

The fields were lumped with hard dirt, which slowed us down. The uneven dirt under my feet caused shooting pains in my bottom, and I tried hard to stay balanced. Sawyer wiggled in his blanket and started to whimper.

"It's okay, honey. Mommy's here. Hang in there just a little bit longer. We're almost to the gravel road. It will be better over there."

His whimpers turned into soft cries. I stopped walking and swung him back and forth, trying to quiet him by talking in hushed tones. I was rewarded with ear piercing screams.

I dropped my backpack and dug out a pre-made bottle. I winced as I lowered myself down on the rough ground, trying to get into a comfortable position. Sawyer only continued to cry, so I popped the bottle in his mouth. He gradually stopped crying and started sucking on the nipple.

While he ate, I surveyed our surroundings. Headlights whizzed past the main road. Traffic came from both sides. It would take hours to walk across these fields, and if we were still walking when the sun came up, we would be spotted immediately. Saint Patrick's already knew we were gone. It was only a matter of time before they started looking for us outside the premises.

Maybe I didn't need to get to the gas station. We were only a hundred yards away from the gravel road that was between two fields. I could walk up the gravel road and find the nearest house and call Jason. He would come and get us. Even if I didn't get to the gas station that Sister Mary Agnes mentioned, eventually the gravel road would lead us somewhere.

The break felt good, but we needed to get going. Sawyer took his time eating, and it took a while to get him to burp. He didn't feel that wet, but I decided to change him anyways. He squirmed as the cool air hit him, but once I wrapped him back in his blankets, he fell right to sleep.

By the time we reached the gravel road, frustrated tears ran down my face. We weren't getting anywhere. Even in the moonlight, I couldn't make out much more than the trees along the ditch. It could be miles before we came upon a house. Dogs barked in the distance. I had come too far just to back pedal to the gas station now.

We must have walked a few miles by now, and Sawyer grew heavier by the minute. Pain settled in my lower back, my shoulders and neck, and my entire lower region was swollen and puffy. It felt like my stitches had ripped open. I desperately need to change my pad, but there were none in the bag. I had to press on.

Finally, headlights appeared on the road ahead. "Yes, yes! Sawyer, someone's coming to help us. Oh, thank God." I stepped into the middle of the road and started waving my one free hand, hoping the driver would stop. The car came to a complete stop a few feet away.

I rushed over and opened the door.

"I bet you never thought you would see me again," the driver said.

A chill went down my spine. It was Sister Mary Eunice.

CHAPTER 23

MACY

"You found him?" I whispered.

"Yes. I have been looking for him for years. I just met him recently."

"You have?"

Jason nodded. "That's what I wanted to talk to you about, if you are still interested."

I rubbed my arms to get the goose bumps to go away. "Oh, I am. I have so many questions. When did you start looking for him? Where did you find him? What does he look like?"

Before Jason could answer, the door flew open and Bree and Ella ran in with Seth following behind them. Seth walked up and put his arm around my waist. "Everything okay?" he asked.

I nodded. "Seth, this is Jason McNally. Jason, this is my husband, Seth." The two men shook hands.

"Nice to meet you. Sorry to hear about your father-in-law," Jason said.

"Likewise, and thank you," Seth replied. He turned to me. "I'm sorry, Macy, I didn't realize anyone

185

else was in here. We didn't mean to intrude. We'll head back into the kitchen. The girls are ready to leave whenever you are." He quickly ushered the two girls away.

"Do you need to go?" Jason asked.

"I probably should," I admitted. "Can we get together to talk before I head back to Los Angeles? I have to drive Seth and the girls back to the airport tonight, but I could find time to get together tomorrow. Would that work for you?"

"Yes, I can make anytime work. I have a lot to share with you."

"Okay, that sounds good. Let me find a pen and paper so I can get your number." I started looking around the church pews.

"Oh, my number hasn't changed. It's still the same as when my grandparents had it. I'm listed in the phone book."

"Alright, I will call you tomorrow." We smiled, and then I watched him walk away. He found him. He found my Sawyer.

***

The girls were livid that they had to return home so soon. Seth and I decided they didn't need to miss any more school or activities, and since the funeral was over, they really had no reason to stay. Elvira would return to the house and make sure that the girls stayed on track. Seth's partners were impatiently waiting for him to return home. They wanted to clear up the Asia Prescott scandal before it got too out of hand, if it hadn't already.

In the midst of packing and the constant whining from the girls, I never got a chance to pull Seth aside and let him know that Jason had found Sawyer. The thought crossed my mind after I dropped them off and we said our goodbyes. I pulled my phone out to send him a text, but I stopped myself. I didn't know what Jason had discovered, and until I did, maybe it wasn't worth mentioning quite yet. Seth had his own messes to deal with, I didn't need to add to it. Well, at least not until I had something concrete.

When the funeral was over, there were a few things to finish up before I headed home for good. I needed to get Dad's clothing and any other personal items from the nursing home. I needed to make sure that the nursing home and funeral were paid, and I wanted to help Brandon and Charlotte write thank you notes for all the sympathy cards we received. Nana's cabin also needed another light cleaning from our stay. Charlotte was busy enough with her four kids, she didn't need to clean up after us.

None of these things should take more than a day or two, but I still didn't book my flight home. Brandon's exhaustion was written all over his face, and more than anything, I wanted to make sure he would be okay. Taking care of these minor things was the least I could do. But still, I couldn't figure out what it was he needed right now that would help him.

Seeing Jason was a welcome distraction. Deep down I really hoped I would run into him again. I was thrilled that he came to both the wake and the funeral. Seeing him at church, I realized that I never truly stopped loving him. And the fact that twenty years later, he found Sawyer, made me realize how much he had loved me, but more importantly, how much he loved our son. The son I couldn't keep. The son I failed to protect.

Was I playing with fire? Was meeting Jason a good idea? Who was I kidding? Jason didn't ask to meet with me to re-kindle our relationship. Twenty years was a long time. I moved on, so there was no reason he wouldn't have moved on himself. Jason only wanted to meet to tell me everything he knew about Sawyer. So why did I keep thinking there was something more to it? Either way, I had no choice but to find out.

***

I was a married woman, a wife, and a mother. So why was I spending over an hour trying to figure out how to do my hair, and struggling with what to wear with my limited wardrobe? I didn't want to admit it, but I wanted him to notice me. I just couldn't explain why I cared after all these years.

Jason had suggested that we meet at a bar or restaurant close by. With all that transpired between Seth and Asia, I decided that meeting somewhere more private would be better. People around town saw the tabloids, and Jason and I whispering in a corner wouldn't look any better. Besides, we had a lot of personal things to catch up on, and I didn't need to do it in the presence of eavesdroppers. It wasn't until after I hung up the phone that I realized how I must have sounded, asking for a private meeting. I hoped he didn't get the wrong idea.

I settled on jeans and a sweatshirt, telling myself I had no one to impress, nor should I. I tamed down the makeup, put a little mousse in my hair and crimped it, just to give it a little volume. I had to stop standing in front of the mirror, or I was going to lose my nerve.

Jason still lived at his grandparents' house on Birch Lake. They were both gone, and the house was gifted to him. He kept them both out of the nursing home, which is what they had wanted. Except for an occasional home-care nurse, Jason took care of everything else. He never left the area, even though my Mother threatened to destroy his reputation. I had no idea what his life had been like since I saw him last.

We agreed to meet at his house for dinner. When I pulled into the driveway, Jason was firing up the grill. He wore an old t-shirt and his faded blue jeans had holes in them. I guess some things hadn't changed. He looked as good as I remembered him, and suddenly I was glad I settled for jeans too.

I rubbed my clammy hands on my jeans, took a deep breath, and got out of the car.

"Hey," was all I could say when I approached.

"Hey yourself," Jason smirked. "You are just in time. The grill is just about ready."

"What are you making?" My stomach clenched tight, I wasn't sure I would be able to eat.

"Steaks, potatoes and some green beans. Can I get you anything to drink? I have water, wine or beer."

"I can grab it," I said. I opened the screen door and stepped inside. He had everything cut, seasoned, and ready on the counter. The table was set for two. He kept the place pretty much the same as when his grandparents owned it. It was tidy and clean, but the pictures and knickknacks and even the furniture were from a different era. He must live here alone. Or maybe he lived somewhere else and he was just using this as a place to meet me.

My hands shook as I grabbed two beers from the fridge. The fridge was full of food, so he couldn't be living anywhere else. Was I really ready for this? Was I ready to face my past head on? Was he as nervous as me? *Shake it off, Macy.* Jason seemed aloof to the whole thing. If I didn't get my act together, and soon, this would end before it ever started.

I tucked the beers in my arm and grabbed the

food. "Ready for the potatoes?" I asked, coming outside with a crooked smile.

"Perfect timing." He grabbed the tin pan from my hands, and I handed him a beer. He cracked it open and took a swig. He motioned to a chair. "Have a seat."

I watched him while he worked the grill. "So…what have you been up to all of these years?"

"Well, after I was fired from Chokecherry, I found some farming jobs over in Holdingford and Melrose. I stayed around here to take care of my grandparents. Now I drive truck, hauling various loads all over the place. I'm not around much anymore. I had this week off," he added.

"Do you have a family?" His life sounded lonely and I knew I had no business asking.

He smiled ruefully. "I'm afraid that ship has sailed. I'm divorced now. I was married for three years. She was a great girl, but…it just didn't work out. She remarried and has a couple of kids now. My parents retired in Arizona. So, I stop there whenever I'm in the area. How is your family doing?"

I shrugged. "Good, I guess. The girls are growing faster than I can keep up. Life in L.A. is busy." I didn't want to talk about Seth or my marriage.

His eyes met mine for a moment. "Are you happy?"

"Y-yes," I stammered as heat rose up my neck and cheeks. He must have seen the tabloids.

He nodded and went back to grilling. "Good," he said.

Should I be offended at such a personal question? "Are you happy?" I asked back, not caring how rude it sounded.

He didn't look up. "I'd like to think so. I wasn't for many years. But I've accepted the fact that life makes its own choices, whether you are ready for it or not."

I sipped on my beer, wondering if he suffered as much as I did.

While Jason finished grilling, we talked about Brandon, Charlotte, and their family, his parents, and mutual friends. We even talked about Leah, and how life had been so tough on her. Jason had heard the same things that I had, and he had run into her from time to time. He thought she looked better than she had in years at my Father's wake, which came as a surprise.

"Are you going to take her up on her invitation and meet with her?" Jason asked as we went inside to eat.

I sighed. "I've been thinking about it since we talked. I truly appreciate her apology, even if it was a long time coming. But our friendship ended twenty years ago. Our lives are a world apart, and I have enough issues as it is. I have a feeling that she has a constant need for drama in her life." Jason agreed.

The smell of the food settled my nerves a little, and I started to relax as we ate.

"Okay, I can't wait anymore. Tell me what you know about our son. What's his name?"

"Charlie. I wondered how long it would take you to bring him up," Jason teased.

"I've been biting my tongue for a while. How long have you been looking for him?"

"Since forever. But in the end, he found me."

My heart nearly burst. "When did this happen?"

"Charlie showed up on my doorstep about a month ago. I get one week off a month and on my first day off, he just showed up. We hung out that week and got to know each other."

A wave of anger and confusion came over me.

"Why am I just finding out about this now?"

"I reached out to you as soon as I could. Before I went back on the road, I stopped over at Brandon's house and asked him for your number. He wanted to know why, so I told him. He was going to call you and see if he had permission to give out your number, but then your Dad went downhill so fast. I really didn't want to do this over the phone. I hated to use your Dad's death as an opportunity, but I knew you would be there. So, at the wake I asked if we could meet. I understood why you turned me down. But I decided during the funeral I wasn't going to let you get away without telling you about this."

I mulled his words over carefully while he put our dishes in the sink. I jumped up and started clearing off the table. "That makes sense. Sorry I jumped the gun."

He waved his hand. "No apology needed. Before I share this with you, I need to know something. This question has plagued me forever. What the hell were you thinking getting in the car with your Mother that day?"

I leaned against the counter and crossed my arms, watching him wash the dishes. "I guess I thought she had calmed down. She was rational, and when she asked me to go to the pharmacy, I thought she was going to apologize for slapping me across the face. I thought, if we were alone in the car, she would listen to me. But she just kept driving and driving. Never, in my wildest dreams, did I suspect that she was capable of doing what she did. She has a vindictive side to her that I had suspected but had never seen, up until that day."

Jason turned the faucet off and turned to face me. "Macy, just so you know, I have never blamed you for what happened. Not once. I hope you know that."

That all too familiar lumped formed in the back of

my throat. I stared at the ground, trying to blink away tears. For twenty years I had pondered that question almost every single day. I buried my face in my hands and started to cry.

Jason kissed the top of my head and wrapped his arms tightly around me.

"How can you even think about forgiving me?" I choked out between sobs. I didn't even care that he saw me ugly cry. "I couldn't save him, Jason. I tried...I tried so hard. I failed miserably. And my life has never been the same."

Chapter 24

Macy

MAY 1994

FARGO, NORTH DAKOTA

I held Sawyer tightly in my arms on the short car ride back. It felt like we had walked miles and miles, when it really must have only been a couple. Maybe I would have had a better chance walking along the ditches on the main road up to the gas station.

Sister Mary Eunice said nothing as I followed her back up to my hospital room. Everything in the room was the same. My suitcase sat open with my clothes shoved on top. My hospital gown lay on my unmade bed. Even my water glass sat on the portable table.

Sister Mary Eunice sat down on a folding chair. I eyed her suspiciously and sat on the bed with Sawyer. She stared me down, and then looked at me in distain.

"Macy, you are bleeding through your clothes. Put the baby on the bed and go change." I didn't move. She sighed. "The doctor will be coming up here to check on both of you once he completes his rounds. It will be a little bit before he gets here. You will still get a chance to say goodbye to the baby."

I really couldn't put it off much longer. I set Sawyer on the bed and went to clean myself up. True

194

to her word, both were still there when I emerged. Sawyer started whimpering again. It had been a few hours since he had eaten, so I dug a bottle out of the backpack.

Sister Mary Eunice peered at the backpack. "Macy, how did you get Sister Mary Agnes' backpack?" The color drained from my face. She grabbed the bag and started removing its contents. "On second thought, how did you manage to sneak into the nursery supply closet on the first floor, and manage to steal bottles, diapers, and wipes? And here's forty-five dollars in cash."

I continued to feed Sawyer, thinking fast. "I stole it. The items were up here in the nursery."

Sister Mary Eunice pursed her lips. "And how did Sister Mary Agnes' backpack manage to get all the way up here?"

Think faster. "Uh, I stole it when we were rooming together. I put it in the bottom of my suitcase."

Just then the doctor and three nurses stepped in. The nurses hovered over the door and over my bed while I continued to feed Sawyer. The doctor pulled up another chair and started asking when Sawyer was fed and changed last, and if I was having any health issues from the extensive walk.

"I need to examine your stitches," he said after he took some notes. I looked down at Sawyer, who was almost done eating. "Take your time," he said.

Sister Mary Eunice cut in. "Macy, I know this is hard on you. And we can all see how much you love your son. But his parents will be here in a couple of hours to take him home. They have been waiting for him for a long time. As hard as this is, you must know that this is the right thing. You are not able to take care of him. Running away and taking a newborn out into the night was not safe. You are not in a clear state of mind right now. However, we decided that we will give you a few more minutes with him, but when he leaves this room, he isn't coming back."

"I don't want to do this. I'm not ready to say goodbye," I whispered.

"In time, you will see that this was the best thing you could have done. He is going to go on and live a happy life with parents who will give him the world. That's why we do this here. We want to give these babies opportunities that they would never have with unwed, high-school aged mothers."

"You get to go home today, Macy. And you graduated early, so you will not have to resume any classes once you return home. We called your Mother when you went missing, and she is already on her way here. Let's end this bad chapter. Let's get you out of here."

I looked down at my son and realized the fight was over. For good this time. We never stood a chance. And now I had to say goodbye to him all over again.

***

I grabbed the college acceptance letters from my desk as I sat down on my bed. I glanced through them, and not one of them sounded like a good fit. They all felt too close to home. I laid down and stared at the ceiling. There was a familiarity in being here, back on Chokecherry farm and in my room. But everything changed now. How I saw my life before Sawyer, was not at all how I saw my life now. I no longer knew who I was. Without Sawyer, I was nothing.

Sawyer was with his new Mom and Dad by now. Two loving parents who would give him a better life than I would. How could that be true? No one would ever love that boy the way I did. I was his Mother. He needed me and not some strangers who knew nothing about him. Would they ever tell him how much I loved him?

There was so much I was going to miss. His first tooth, coos, and giggles. Skinned knees from riding his bike for the first time. His first haircut, his first day of school, hearing him read a book for the first time. I would miss holidays, birthdays and all his accomplishments. He was going to grow from an infant to a toddler, from a young boy to a man. He had a whole life to live, without me in it.

I turned to my side and hugged my pillow. I spotted my unopened suitcase sitting up against my closet. I sat up abruptly. *Could it be?* I jumped out of bed, ripped open the suitcase, and dumped all its contents on the floor. I felt around until I found the tear in the lining. *Please God…*

And then I felt them. My two Polaroid pictures were still there! I could see him. I could see my baby boy every single day. Even though he would never know who I was, I would never have to forget his little features, like his little button nose. My Mother could try to erase him all she wanted, but this was my proof that he existed. Given my current circumstances, this was more than I ever could have dreamed of.

That night, with my pictures under my pillow, I thought of my precious boy and imagined me holding him. As I drifted off to sleep, I could have sworn that I heard the faint sound of Jason's pickup truck, over at Willow's Pond.

***

"This was a bad idea," I said, grabbing my luggage off the conveyer belt.

"Well, bad decisions become the best memories. You've been studying way too hard lately. You deserve this break," Savannah said while she scanned the luggage tags. "If my bag doesn't come soon, I'll be wearing all your swimsuits."

I laughed in spite of myself. "Too bad you're too fat to wear any of my clothes." Savannah, my college roommate for the past three years, was at least two sizes smaller than me. My clothes would fall off her.

"Oh, here it is," she said, struggling to pull it off the belt. She must have packed a month's worth of clothes. "My aunt set up a driver to take us to the beach house. He should be parked outside."

Savannah's aunt and uncle were working in Europe for a few months. They graciously agreed to let us use their house in Panama City, Florida. My student loans were adding up fast, but since we only had to pay for airfare, it was a no brainer. Rates were reasonable, and a week on the beach was just what I needed.

The driver shuttled us to the liquor store and grocery store before the beach house. The house stood tall and gorgeous in the sunlight. I had never seen a house on stilts before. Every window had a view of the water. *I could live here forever*, I decided while standing on the balcony. I had never stayed in such a large room before. I had my own bathroom, too. The closet was the size of the dorm room I shared with Savannah. This was picture perfect. A little slice of heaven.

We got in our swimsuits and headed to the beach. The white sand burned my feet while we found a place to put our towels. The waves crashed softly along the shore, surrounding me with peace.

"I think the ocean waves could put me to sleep. Either that or this strawberry daiquiri could," I said, taking a sip.

Savannah laughed. "Well rest up now, because there are house parties all along the beach here. We are going to hit them up, starting tonight."

For once in my life, it felt great to feel so free. Maybe Savannah was right. This week away was just what I needed.

***

Music drifted from the backyards of beach houses as we strolled along the beach that evening. Strings of lights surrounded decks and patios. And in between it all, the ocean waves crashed into the sand. Lovers held hands as they walked along the shore, and there were some Frisbee and football games going on along the beach.

"Let's stop at this house," Savannah said. "There are people dancing."

"Okay," I said, suddenly nervous about party crashing.

"Oh, let loose a little, Macy. This is what spring break in Panama City is about." I had to trust her as she had done this several times before.

Savannah pranced her way onto the deck and started dancing with everyone else. No one seemed to care or notice, so I casually made my way to her. I had never been dancing before, except for a seventh-grade dance. Savannah had sexy moves, while I moved rather clumsily. I tried to match everyone else's moves, but I knew I looked like an idiot.

Savannah had been dancing with the same guy for a while. I eyed the keg and bowed out to go get a beer. All the seats circling the dancers were full, so I walked down the steps to the beach, and sat in the sand.

Within minutes the couple next to me started making out. Their hands were all over each other, and when they started moaning, I got up and walked to the pier.

I walked all along the pier, taking in the salt water smell, and observing the seagulls flying around. I couldn't get enough of the ocean, and the moonlight beamed down on the water, making it more beautiful in the darkness. I sat down on the bench at the end, taking it all in, while sipping my lukewarm beer. After a while, I decided that I should probably go check in with Savannah. The pier had cleared out by then, and just as I was about to get up, someone sat down next to me.

"Hi," he said.

"Hello."

"You have an accent. Where are you from?" he asked.

"Minnesota. Well, I live in Chicago now."

"You must be here for spring break."

I nodded. "Aren't you here for spring break?"

"I am," he said. "I have to admit, I'm a first timer. I don't know all the rules yet."

"Me neither," I said. "In fact, I was at a party, waiting for my friend, but then this couple next to me started groping each other, so I came here for a while. Are you here with friends?"

"Yeah, my buddy, Nate. He was the guy sitting next you," he said, grinning.

I spit out my beer and burst out laughing. I covered my mouth, but that only made me laugh harder.

"You're in for a long night if you plan to wait for him. What's your name?" I asked.

"Seth. Seth Whitaker."

***

Seth and I sat on that pier bench in Panama City for hours, slowly getting to know each other. Seth lived in California and was studying to become a lawyer. Like me, this was his first spring break vacation, and he felt guilty for taking the time off, instead of studying for his exams. Seth and his friend Nate rented a house just a few houses from where we were staying.

Savannah found us a few hours later. She was obviously drunk and needed assistance getting back to our house.

"Can I see you again?" Seth asked as I stood to leave. For some reason, Jason and Sawyer came to my mind as soon as he asked.

But what the hell? It wouldn't hurt spending time with him. He lives in California, so after this week we would never see each other again. "Sure," I found myself saying. "You know where I live."

***

Seth and I were inseparable for the duration of our break. We didn't leave the beach once. We walked the beach, talked on the piers, and visited house parties. Savannah had found someone special, too, and occasionally we would all eat at a seafood dive that was within walking distance.

By the time our vacation came to an end, I grew conflicted. Seth was a great guy, and he made it obvious that he wanted something more after Panama City. Was I ready for that? Then I remembered what Nana always said. She always gave two pieces of advice, when it came to finding a mate.

"Always remember this," she would say. "There are only two things you need to look for in a boyfriend that could potentially turn into a husband. Number one: Be smarter than him. And number two, which is the most important: Make sure he loves you more than you love him. That way, he will never hurt you."

I certainly wasn't smarter than Seth. History already proved that, and he was going to be a lawyer. But he was more into me than I was into him. Sadly, that's because my heart belonged to two other boys that used to be in my life. Before I let whatever this is go any further, or before I developed any real feelings, I needed to see how he truly felt about me. If I had learned anything about what happened to me, I learned that when you have secrets, you have nothing.

On our last night together, I pulled two Polaroid's out of my purse, wondering if I would ever hear from Seth Whitaker again.

***

I graduated with an Economics degree from the University of Chicago in 1998. The next day, I flew to Los Angeles, California, for my wedding day. Wearing blue jeans, Seth and I stood in front of a judge at the court house and became husband and wife. Only Savannah and Nate were invited, and they served as our witnesses.

I mailed a note and a copy of our marriage license to my Mother. I had not spoken to her since the day she dropped me off at Saint Patrick's. That last summer I was home I ignored her completely. I only responded to my Dad and Brandon, if I had to. I applied to the University of Chicago, and once I was accepted, I made plans to never return. I never came home for breaks or holidays. I applied for odd jobs, worked my way through school, and rented a place to stay for the summer to avoid going home.

My measly earnings didn't cover everything though. I graduated with mountains of student debt, and Seth was still finishing up law school. We rented a little studio apartment, and I got to work right away. I found a daytime job as a secretary, and on nights and weekends I waitressed. The pay wasn't great, but it paid the rent, utilities and the minimum payments on my student loans. We didn't have much, but we had each other, and we had our big dreams.

Mother sent a note back a few weeks later, congratulating us on our marriage and my graduation. She said she wanted to meet Seth and asked me to call her. I tossed the note in the garbage, refusing to give it a second thought.

Seth was elated a few months later when I told him I was pregnant. Horrifying memories came rushing back, and my panic attacks started coming on a regular basis. I had constant dreams of my baby being taken away again. I could smell the musty odor of the rooms at the convent, which woke me from fitful sleeps. The insomnia got so bad that eventually Seth made me tell the doctor.

At our twelve-week appointment, the doctor confirmed my fears.

"I'm so sorry," she said. "But I can't find a heartbeat."

I never heard the rest of the conversation. She prescribed an anti-depressant and recommended therapy. I didn't hear Seth tell her how I had been acting or why I was in a constant state of fear.

That same hollow feeling was back. But this time, I knew why. My Mom had been right all along. God was punishing me for all my past sins.

***

By the time Bree came along, we were in a better spot both financially and mentally. Therapy and the pills helped me return to some sort of normalcy. Seth had graduated law school and found a job. We moved from a studio to a two-bedroom apartment and we were able to make double student loan payments.

I called my parents to let them know when Bree had arrived, safe and sound. They didn't know about the miscarriage. They did know about this pregnancy as I sent them a note and a picture of an ultrasound when I was six months along. The doctor finally convinced me that this pregnancy wouldn't end the way the last one did. Although I was scared that I was going to lose yet another baby, I decided to take my chances and tell my parents. Mother sent back a congratulations card with a package of baby items.

"She's here," I said on the day of Bree's delivery. I tried to sound upbeat on the phone. Even though we were thousands of miles away, the idea that she knew my baby was here, terrified me.

There was a long pause on the other end of the line. Mother's voice cracked. "Oh, Macy. A *real* baby. Oh, I can't wait to see her. Please send me some pictures right away. When will you bring her to see Grandma and Grandpa?"

I had no answer for her.

CHAPTER 25
MACY

My eyes were puffy and swollen as we sat back down at the kitchen table. We forgot about the dishes soaking in the sink.

"After I saw you and your Mom on the road, I didn't park at our spot right away. I didn't want to give away our meeting place. So, I drove around, waiting for you guys to return. I waited for hours before going home."

"I showed up the next day, not knowing what I was walking into. I figured I would play it off as though I was coming to work, until I could see you and get another game plan. When I got there, Howard met me at my pickup. He said he was so disappointed in us. He had no idea we had taken things so far. He told me he had no choice but to let me go. I asked him where you were, but he wouldn't tell me."

"Was Mother there?" I asked.

Jason shook his head. "Not that day. Howard wouldn't tell me where you had gone or when you would be back. Every night I parked in the woods, hoping you would come out. After a week of you not showing up, I started calling. Elaine would answer, tell me you were unavailable, and she would hang up before I could respond. After a couple of weeks, I drove back there, demanding to know where you were. Elaine laughed in my face, and told me if I ever called there again, or if they ever saw my pickup again, they would file an Order for Protection. I cried, begged, and pleaded, but nothing worked. Finally, Elaine said that you wanted to leave town so you wouldn't have to deal with me. She said that you wanted to give the baby up for adoption, but you were too afraid of me, so you had to leave town for your own protection." Jason ran his hand through his hair and sighed.

"I knew none of that was true. But I couldn't figure out where you had gone. I had no hope of finding out either. You weren't speaking with Leah, and we were the only two who knew about the baby until your Mom found out, so there was no one else to ask."

I stared at him, tears falling down my cheeks. "I'm sorry. I didn't know any of this."

Jason squeezed my hands from across the table. "I know you didn't. Eventually I knew you weren't coming back, and I was running out of money. So, I found a farm job in Melrose and started working there. About five years later I got a letter in the mail. Do you recall Sister Mary Agnes?"

My eyes grew wide. "Yes! She was the closest person I had at the convent. She tried to help us escape."

Jason smiled. "I figured you would remember. So out of the blue I get this letter from her. She said that she had information that she thought I would like to know about you and the baby. She provided her phone number and said that she would be open to a phone call or to meet sometime for coffee."

"I can't believe the convent let her contact you," I said. "Sister Mary Eunice was so strict that she would never have allowed that to happen. She read all the incoming and outgoing mail."

"I called Sister Mary Agnes that same night. It turns out Sister Mary Eunice questioned her on you running away when you left. Sister Mary Agnes confessed to everything, and she was kicked out of the church."

I sat back in my chair and ran my hands through my hair. "She lost everything…because of me."

Jason shook his head. "Macy, she said you helped her figure out her own dreams. She was devastated at first. But then she got married and now she has four kids. She is happier than ever and says that she would never have been able to live out her life the way she wanted if it weren't for you. Her family pushed her to be a nun, and she didn't want to disappoint them."

I exhaled slowly. "Wow, I had no idea. This is…incredible. What made her decide to contact you?"

"She said she sent some letters to your parent's house. They were all returned, unopened. She didn't know of any other way to reach you, but she remembered my name and decided to write me and see what happened. She wanted to know what happened to both of us.

She shared everything from the night you got there, to breaking into the office to call me for help. How she had to babysit you until you had the baby. She said, when she saw how much you loved that boy, she couldn't sit around and do nothing. She had to help."

"She was a phenomenal woman," I muttered, still

blown away.

"She still is. After she told me everything, I drove up to meet her in Fargo. We went to the convent to get the adoption records. We just wanted the parents' names so we could try to connect with them. My plan wasn't to try to take Charlie away from his parent's or do anything stupid. I just wanted to meet him and let him know who I was. The convent slammed the door in our faces."

"I'm not at all surprised. Did you know that I named our baby Sawyer? It was a name you had liked."

Jason smiled. "I know, and I loved it. Sister Mary Agnes told me. Just so you know, she changed her name when she was kicked out of the convent. Her name is now Heather."

"Heather, huh? That suits her. Oh, I have missed her. So, what did you do when they wouldn't release the files?"

"Well, we did nothing that day. We went for lunch and discussed what she had seen behind closed doors. She explained about all of the "donations" that came from the unwed mother's families, and the "donations" for the new parents adopting the babies. It's total coercion. There were very few pregnant mothers who wanted to be there. I started taking notes. After that we set up weekly phone calls and would discuss anything she could remember. She remembered some of the names of the girls who were in there. I interviewed a few of them. Unfortunately, she didn't know who any of the adoptive parents were, as she was never privy to those records."

"Once I felt we had gathered up enough evidence, we went to the local newspaper in Fargo with all our information. The reporter ate this all up, and within the next few days, it made front page news. Soon local television crews were on their door steps, demanding answers. After that, some unwed mothers also wanted answers."

I shook my head in disbelief. "And I was in California by then. I ran as far and as fast as I could. Yet, this whole time, you were taking on the convent head on. Why couldn't I be more like you?" Bringing up the convent brought back a lot of painful memories. That all too familiar knot in my stomach was back.

"I never set out to do any of this, Macy. It just sorta…happened. I didn't want anyone else to go through this. Heather felt like she got the justice that all of you deserved. She was hurt by this whole process, too. Both of us did interviews at radio stations and we were on the news once. The unwed mothers program shut down shortly after that. The church lost a lot of money. Sister Mary Eunice stepped down and another nun took her place. The church held their ground, though. Their lawyer had answers for all of the money in question."

"I am so glad that place has shut down now. That convent has haunted me for years. So how did all of this bring you to Sawyer— er, Charlie, I mean?"

"I've always known him as Sawyer, too. It took a little bit to get used to Charlie. So, after I shared my story, nothing happened for a long time. Once the program shut down, there was nothing else I could do. They still didn't release the records, so I had nothing to go on. I moved on with my life as best I could."

"About a year ago, my parents started talking about websites where you can submit your DNA. They were doing it to find out what their ethnic background was. I looked into it and realized that you can also do it to connect with other relatives. So, I submitted it to several different websites."

"A few weeks before Charlie showed up, I got a hit on one of the sites. Charlie was looking for us, too. He went to the convent for answers and hadn't gotten anywhere. He remembered seeing me on the news, although he didn't know who I was. He and his parents were sick about it. We messaged back and forth a few times. I didn't expect him to show up on my doorstep though. He said he wanted to drive by, but when he saw my pickup in the yard, he decided to go for it."

"Where does he live? What does he do?" I wanted to know everything.

"He grew up in Fargo, but now lives in Saint Cloud. He is in his second year of school at Saint Cloud State University. He plays hockey and got in on a hockey scholarship. He's staying in the dorms."

"What's he like?" I asked.

"Smart, amazing…cute, like his Mom." Jason laughed.

I blushed. "All I have of him are my two pictures. Let me show you…" I looked around for my purse, and then realized I left it in the car. "Let me go get them." I went to the car to grab my purse. As I headed back in, I peeked at my phone.

I had six missed calls from Seth, and two text messages. The first message said, '*Where are you?*' And the second one said '*Macy, it's bad. Asia sold the other photos. Please call me.*' I stopped cold. Ugh, this is not what I needed right now. I regretted even looking at my phone. I shot him a text back. '*This is not my problem. Figure out your shit as I am figuring out mine.*' I shut my phone off before temptation got the better of me. Now was not the time to start an Internet search.

"You okay?" Jason asked as I walked back in.

I nodded. I moved my chair closer so we could see

the worn and faded Polaroid's together. "Sister Mary—Heather, I guess I should now call her. She snuck a camera up in my room and took these two pictures. I hid them in the lining of my suitcase, and no one ever found them. These two pictures are what got me through that terrible ordeal and everything after it. I slept with these pictures under my pillow for years. Now I keep them on my nightstand, but I brought them with me since I didn't know how long I was going to be here."

Jason looked at the pictures for a long time. His eyes clouded over for a moment. "I'm so sorry I wasn't there, Macy. I should have been. I wish we could go back and do this whole thing over again."

I thought about that for a minute. "For a long time, I did too. But then, I wouldn't have had my girls."

"Yeah, you would have. You would have had them with me." Our eyes met as he put his hand on my leg and slowly leaned in. I pressed my forehead against his and ran my fingers through his hair.

"Jason," I whispered. I kissed him passionately and hard, wanting, no—needing, more. He kissed me back with the same fierceness, pulling me closer. He lifted me onto the table, and I wrapped my legs around him. I rubbed my hands up and down his chest and felt him shudder with anticipation. His hands went under my sweatshirt and I moaned as he cupped my breasts.

"Jason," I said breathlessly, pulling myself away. "We have to stop. I can't do this…"

"Why not?" He frowned.

I stared at his chest, not able to meet his eyes. "Well, for starters, I'm married."

"Yeah, I know that. I also know that's not stopping your husband. I've seen his pictures with that movie star."

I looked away, wanting to jump off the table, but he was blocking me. "It's not what it looks like. Asia Prescott is blackmailing my husband, and if he doesn't...you know what, never mind. It doesn't matter."

"I think it does matter, Macy. You can't honestly believe that nothing is going on between them." He backed up so I could get off the table.

"I don't know what I believe. But I need time to figure it out, and this isn't the way to do it."

"We never finished where we left off. We never ended, Macy, and I know you know that. We were supposed to be together. We had a future. Don't tell me you forgot that. Don't tell me it didn't mean anything to you."

"You meant everything to me," I yelled. "You have no idea how much I loved you. But I paid the ultimate price. I lost everything and everyone because of it. But that was twenty years ago. Eventually I had to move on with my life. You did too, Jason. You were married."

"And why do you think that didn't work out?"

"Are you telling me I am the cause of your divorce?" I asked.

"No, I was the cause of my divorce. But that's because I couldn't get you and Charlie out of my mind. I shut down, and when I went on this crusade to shut down the convent, she walked out. I hurt her deeply, and I will always regret that. But having you stand here in my kitchen, kissing me like you just were, tells me that I know I am not crazy. You are feeling this too, Macy. I could *feel* it."

"It's not that simple, Jason. Not only do I have a husband, but I have two kids. Our life is in California. Did you think that I was just going to walk back in here and leave the life I worked so hard to build? That I would fall right into your arms and we would pick up where we left off twenty years ago?"

Jason sat down on the chair and looked out the window. Then he sighed. "I don't know what I thought. I wasn't thinking those things before you got here. But when you got here, I realized that I never stopped loving you. I'm sorry I gave into those feelings." He looked at me tearfully. "Don't you see the injustice of it all? We were supposed to be together. You, me and Charlie. We had our whole future ripped away from us. It wasn't supposed to turn out like this."

"I know. There isn't a day that goes by that I don't wonder what our life would have been like had my Mother not interfered. But I can't keep living in the past. My past haunted me to the point of thinking about suicide. I had to let go. I had no other choice." My eyes filled with tears.

"You had to let go of me?"

"Well...I certainly had to try."

We sat there silently, neither of us sure of what to say next. Our feelings had been buried for twenty years and we could no longer ignore them. I broke the ice first.

"So...how can I get a hold of Charlie? I would like to see him before I go home."

Jason went into the living room and returned with a piece of paper. "This is his phone number. He knows everything that has happened, from the time we met until now. I didn't hold anything back. He knows that you are here tonight, and he said that I am supposed to text him and let him know what your thoughts are. But you can certainly do that on your own."

"Thank you," I said, caressing the paper as if it were gold. "This means a lot. Do you have Heather's number as well?"

He went back into the living room. When he returned, he hesitated as he handed me the piece of paper. "I put my cell phone number on there, too. In case you ever need it."

"Jason, I want you to know how much I appreciate everything you have done for…us over the years. I only wish that I would have known sooner. I didn't think that I could ever face you again. I thought you hated me for not being able to save Charlie." I stood to leave.

"Macy, I could never hate you. The only thing I ever wanted in this life was to love you the way you deserved."

I squeezed his arm, knowing I would lose all control if I hugged him again. "Goodnight, Jason."

"Take care, Macy."

By the time I got to my car I was balling uncontrollably. The heartbreak was just as strong as it was twenty years ago. For some reason, it felt like I was saying goodbye to Jason all over again.

CHAPTER 26

JASON

April 2014
Grey Eagle, Minnesota

"Are you happy?" What the hell kind of question is that, and why did I feel the need to ask it? I blurted it out so fast, before I realized how it sounded. I saw the surprised look on her face as she squirmed in her seat. I had no right to ask her that.

Maybe it was seeing that pompous ass at the funeral that made me ask such a personal question. Watching him put his hand on the small of her back stirred feelings in me that I hadn't felt in a long time. He didn't deserve her, and there was plenty of proof of that.

I offered to meet her in public so she wouldn't feel uncomfortable. She'd already turned down a meeting once and I didn't dare risk it a second time. When Macy suggested someplace more private, I knew she wouldn't back out on me again. Especially since I told her about Charlie.

Thankfully she showed up. I held my breath as she got out of the car. I'm not sure how, but Macy was more beautiful than she was twenty years ago. My eyes lingered on her tight jeans that hugged all the right places. *That's enough, McNally. Remember she's married and has no interest in you. That ship has sailed.*

Macy looked like a ghost when she came in with the Polaroid's. From the window, I watched her grab her phone and abruptly stop. Her face paled as she wrote something back and shoved her phone back in her purse. It didn't take a rocket scientist to figure out that her husband had something to do with her sudden change. She felt...colder, as she came in.

I had no right to kiss her, and I can't even say why I did it. It just felt...right. When she ran her fingers through my hair and pulled me to her, I knew she wanted me as much as I wanted her. And she smelled so damn good. I had no intentions of stopping, either. I wanted to rip those clothes off and make up for lost time.

I shouldn't have been surprised when she pulled away, but I was. Macy is the most committed person I have ever met. Even though her douche bag husband hurt her, she had way too much class for cheap revenge sex.

Feeling rejected, I hurled insults about her husband and marriage. What kind of man would do such a thing? And then when I implied that she was the leading cause of my divorce...Ugh, what was I thinking?

I acted like a horny teenager and then had the nerve to pick a fight when she turned me down. I guess I am no better than her husband after all. I blew it. She came over for one reason only—Charlie.

Even though she wasn't mine to lose, it felt like I was losing her all over again. It hurt just as bad today as it did twenty years ago. But now that she was in my life

again, I couldn't bear the thought of never seeing her
again.

Chapter 27
Macy

Nana's small cabin sparkled by the time I got done cleaning it – again. Cleaning calmed my nerves and kept my hands busy. Charlie was on his way over to Chokecherry to meet me for the first time, and I was terrified. *Was he mad at me for not being able to rescue him? What if he doesn't like me?*

It was my last day at Chokecherry. I wanted to stay longer so I could spend more time with Charlie, but this was the only day he had available. Tomorrow I would fly back home to Los Angeles to resume my life, as if there was any way to do that now. I wasn't the same person I was just a few short weeks ago. This trip changed everything. Brandon and I were closer than we have ever been. I finally felt like I got to know his family. Being around Jason made me realize that I never stopped loving him, and I never will. It was time to put him behind me and finally move forward. But the best part of this whole trip was meeting my son for the first time.

Adrenaline and nausea pumped through me all morning, as I packed and cleaned the entire cabin. As I saw Charlie's rusty white Pontiac turn into the driveway, I broke out in a sweat. *I should have put on more deodorant*, I thought as I fanned my damp shirt.

By the time I got to Charlie's car he was already out. He stood taller than me, and he was wearing a hockey t-shirt, jeans and a baseball cap. As I neared him, he smiled and took off his sunglasses.

I sucked in my breath as I stared at him. He was beautiful. He looked so much like Jason it took my breath away. Charlie had the same dirty blond hair and ocean blue eyes as Jason did. He had my smile. He was the perfect combination of both of us.

Unwelcomed tears blurred my eyes and I tried to blink them away. "It's so nice to finally meet you," was all I could manage to say.

He opened his arms for a hug, and I leaned into him, crying. Maybe I was crying because he was standing in front of me, or because I missed twenty years of his life, or because it hurt so badly, yet it was so wonderful, all at once.

When I looked up, he had tears in his eyes, too. "I have waited my whole life for this. I'm so glad it's finally happening," he said.

"I'm sorry, I'm just – just so happy. Come inside," I said, grabbing his hand. "I have so many questions. I want to know everything I missed for the past twenty years."

"Well, that could take a while…" he said.

I laughed. "I've got all the time in the world."

We settled on the rocking chairs in the living room. "When do you go back to L.A.?" Charlie asked.

"I go back tomorrow. I have been here for a few weeks and it's time to get back home. You have two sisters, Bree and Ella. They don't know about you yet, but they will. Do you have a big family?"

Charlie shook his head. "I'm an only child. My Mom and Dad couldn't afford to adopt again."

"Does that bother you?"

"It used to. For years I asked for a brother or a sister. I couldn't understand why they didn't have any more children when everyone else around me did. But now I understand."

I could listen to his voice forever. "Have you always known you were adopted? What are your parents like?"

"Yes, I have known since I could remember. My parents were told by the convent that my birth father was unknown, and my birth mother was raped, and she didn't want me, so I was put up for adoption. Once the convent stuff came out, my parents no longer believed that, and they pushed me to find out the truth. They have supported me in every way. They would like to meet you and Jason. They said any family of mine is their family, too."

"I would like that. Sounds like they have been good to you. That means so much to me, Charlie. I prayed for years that you were in a good home. How did you feel about being adopted?"

"Sometimes it made me angry, thinking that I was a product of rape. And that you didn't want me. I love my parents very much, but I always knew I came from somewhere else. All I wanted when I submitted my DNA was just to find out where I came from. And here I am."

I showed him the two Polaroid pictures. "I slept with the pictures under my pillow for years. Now I always keep them on my nightstand, but I brought them with me since I knew I would be here for a while."

Charlie studied them. "Jason told me what he

knew about your days at the convent. I can't believe you tried to escape with me. It was a relief to know that you guys did love me."

I smiled. "I don't know why I thought I would get away with it, but I had to try. I fought against them the whole time. I never wanted to let you go, Charlie. I love you so much. But I do feel bad that Sister Mary Agnes, well Heather now, got in trouble because of it. But Jason said she went on to become a Mom and is happy with her life."

"I met her," Charlie said. "She's a great gal and she told me everything she could remember. She has always wondered what happened to you."

"I will call her when I return home. I can't wait to connect with her. To think, after all these years, she still thinks about us. She's a remarkable woman. So, Jason tells me you play hockey?"

"Yes, I got a hockey scholarship at SCSU. It keeps me busy. I'm in my second year. My parents show up to almost every game."

I hugged him tightly. "Charlie, I'm so glad that your life turned out as well as it has. You have parents that love and support you, and you are doing what makes you happy. Do you think that after today, you will want to keep in touch? Is there any way that I could have a part in your life now, even if it's a small one? I've gone twenty years without you, and I can't have you leave knowing it could be another twenty years before I see you again."

"I think I'd like that very much."

"Good," I sighed in relief. "Can you stay for dinner? I'll show you around the farm. My brother Brandon, his wife Charlotte, and their four kids live in the main house. They can't wait to meet you."

***

Meeting Charlie filled a twenty-year long dream. We had a wonderful evening together, and everyone enjoyed getting to know him. As hard as it was to see him go, I knew it wouldn't be forever. This was just the beginning. I hugged him long and hard before he left, and we promised to keep in touch. I couldn't wait to tell his sisters about him.

I was still reminiscing when I got to the airport. I happily floated around the airport, until a convenient store magazine rack stopped me in my tracks. Seth hadn't lied about the pictures, although they were worse than I imagined. The tabloids gracing the stands were of my husband, yet again with Asia Prescott. This time they were kissing passionately, and he was embracing her half naked body. The caption read *'Affair with married lawyer has been going on for months.'*

My heart sank as I stared at the picture. Seth didn't look surprised or angry about the ordeal as he claimed. In fact, the way his hands were placed on her hips and lower back showed me that they had been enjoying themselves for a while before the photo was taken. Whether Asia blackmailed Seth was neither here nor there anymore. There was more to this relationship than Seth let on. Why was he lying to me about it, especially knowing that these pictures were going to be tabloid fodder?

I supposed I would call it a moment of weakness, but I found myself buying that stupid magazine. I flipped through the pages until I found the article. There were three other photos. Seth's hands were in different positions in all of them. I studied those pictures until I boarded the plane. As the plane started to ascend, Jason's words echoed in my head. "The only thing I ever wanted in this life was to love you the way you deserved." Why was my life so damn complicated?

***

Elvira, Bree and Ella were in the kitchen, waiting for me to walk in the door. The girls had 'Welcome Home' signs in their hands, and they cheered and gave me a hug when I walked in. Elvira made lasagna and garlic bread for supper, so that I could catch up with the girls.

Seth came in from the veranda when he heard the commotion. He hovered a few feet away, unsure of what to do or say. I hadn't responded to any more of his messages or phone calls in Minnesota. He looked like he hadn't showered or shaved in a few days, and his hair stood on all ends, as though he had been running his hands through it several times.

Elvira glared at him, and then she grabbed her purse to go. "Thank you so much for my trip to Mexico, Senora Whitaker," she said, giving me another hug. "It is good to have you home."

"You're welcome," I said, hugging her tightly. "I appreciate everything you have done for us, especially these past few weeks. I didn't have to worry about the girls once, knowing that you were here. I'll see you tomorrow." Elvira beamed.

The girls didn't leave my side the rest of the evening. They wanted to share everything that I had missed, and they wanted to know how Brandon, Charlotte and the kids were doing, and when they could see them again.

Without waiting to discuss it with Seth, I took the photos out of my purse. "Do you girls remember when I said I would tell you all about these pictures someday?" They nodded as Seth watched from the sofa. "Well, today's the day to tell you about them. The little baby in this picture is my baby. His name is Charlie, and he is your older brother."

Seth sat up straight and shook his head. "Really, Macy…"

I cut him off. "Twenty years ago, when I was in high-school, I got pregnant. I had a baby, and he was placed for adoption. And I got to meet him for the first-time last night."

"I have a brother?" Ella asked.

Bree crossed her arms and furrowed her brows. "Why are you just telling us this now? How come we didn't get to meet him?"

"Well, your dad and I weren't sure how to tell you, although I have wanted to tell you about him for a long time. I didn't know that I was going to meet him until two nights ago, and you were already back home by then. Charlie really wants to meet you. He said he never grew up with sisters and he can't believe that he has two now." I pulled my cell phone out and pulled up a picture. "This is what he looks like today."

"Did you show him a picture of us?" Ella asked.

"Of course, I did. He has never been to California. He might come and visit us someday. Or, we can go back to Minnesota and visit him. He is a hockey player in college. Maybe we can go watch one of his games sometime."

Seth stormed out of the room.

"I can't believe you never told me," Bree said, crossing her arms.

"I'm sorry, honey. I hope you can forgive me and see how special this is. You have a big brother now."

"Well, I didn't ask for one." She ran upstairs to her room. I cringed when the door slammed. This was not the reaction I expected to receive, although I should have. This was life changing news. I started to get up, and then decided against it. Maybe she needed a little more time to digest this information before talking it out.

"I think it's cool," Ella said.

I laughed. "Me too, kiddo. Now, come and give me another hug."

***

Exhaustion set in by the time I got the girls to bed. I hauled my luggage upstairs and dropped it in the doorway to our room. Seth was furiously pacing the floor.

"You had no right to tell the girls about him without consulting me first." I ignored him and walked into the bathroom. He followed. "I'm serious, Macy. You've got some nerve, coming home after all this time, and dropping a bombshell-."

I cut him off. "A bombshell? You want a BOMBSHELL?" I stormed passed him and went to my purse, throwing the magazine at him. "This is a bombshell, Seth. I actually believed your sad, pathetic story. You were not a victim, Seth. Your hands were all over her. You are a lying son of a bitch."

"Let's talk about lying, Macy. You turned your phone off and wouldn't speak to me. I called over to your brother's house to make sure you were okay. Charlotte said you were meeting with a friend. Hmm, it doesn't take a rocket scientist to figure out what 'friend' you were seeing. Obviously, you were with Jason. Then you walk in the door and tell the girls all about your son, when you promised we would do it when the time was right."

"The time is right, right now! Yes, I saw Jason. We had dinner together. I wasn't going to lie to you about it. Charlie found him, and he wanted to tell me about it. That's a little different than that," I said, pointing to the magazine in Seth's hands.

Seth threw the magazine on the floor. "You had to have a whole dinner just for him to tell you that they found each other? You can't tell me it wasn't something more. There just aren't any pictures to prove it."

"You're right, there is more to that. A lot more. Twenty years of things that we had to catch up on. He was an important part of my life. And you want to know what else? He said he is still in love with me, even after all these years. But I'm married, Seth. That means something to me, even if it doesn't mean anything to you."

"It does mean something to me," he sighed. He sat down at the edge of the bed.

"Until Asia Prescott?"

Seth ran his hands through his hair. "Yes. No...I guess so."

"How long has this been going on?" I demanded, suddenly scared to learn the truth.

"It started a few months before her divorce was settled. I figured it wouldn't last long. That she would move on before it got too out of hand."

"How could you do that to me? How many other affairs have there been?" I asked.

"This is the only one. I don't know why I did it, Macy. It just happened. We were working long hours together and one thing led to another. I guess it was fun and exciting and she...she's just different."

"Wow. I'm sorry that I'm the boring wife. So, while I have been taking care of your children, you have been cheating on me. So now what? Are you still seeing her?"

He shrugged. "I guess so. It was never supposed to get this complicated. Macy, I still love you. I'm so sorry. I never meant to hurt you."

"You *guess* so? You accuse me of doing something wrong for having dinner with Jason and you have been sleeping with Asia for *months*. This is incredible. What does everyone at the firm think of your affair?"

"They let me go when I confessed. I don't have a job and I don't know if I ever will. They gave me a six-month severance if I left right then and there."

"So, are you going to leave her?" My voice cracked. "Or are you going to leave me?"

He was silent for far too long. "I think I have to see where this goes." He hung his head. "I never thought it would go this far. You have to know that."

I yanked my pillow off the bed and headed into the spare bedroom. Never had Nana's words rang so true as now: Make sure he loves you more than you love him. That way he will never hurt you.

I guess I had been wrong all along.

CHAPTER 28
MACY

My eyes were bloodshot and puffy when I woke. It took a second to get my bearings, and when I realized where I was, I buried my face in my pillow. How did I get here? What the hell was I supposed to do now?

Was I supposed to smack Seth across the face or pour a glass of wine on him? Maybe I should have torn up his clothes or thrown them all out in the street. Or, I should have grabbed Seth's phone, called up Asia and gave her a piece of my mind. Maybe I should have screamed at her, told her to stay the hell away from my husband and threatened her.

I should have known that he was cheating. I should have seen the signs. Looking back, they were there, and I missed them. He would come home late and hop in the shower before he would even say hello. He started working out more and wore sexier boxers, even though he was too tired to make love in the evenings. Slowly, he had distanced himself, and I was too busy to even notice.

After fifteen years together, this is how it's going to

end? Would it have ended had those pictures not shown up? Those pictures were a punch to the gut, and I have never been more humiliated. Our personal business is now front-page news. Sometime soon, my daughters would see them or hear about them too.

I gathered my belongings and put them away before the girls woke up. Seth wasn't in our bed. It was still made so Seth either didn't get any sleep, or he snuck out to be with Asia. I guess it didn't matter either way.

Tough decisions were going to have to be made. Seth didn't want to fix our marriage and I would never be able to trust him again. I met him in the kitchen, where he was waiting with fresh coffee. As I studied his guilt-ridden face, I wondered if I ever truly knew him at all. We had been through so much together, but I no longer knew him. If I called a spade a spade, he was most likely thinking the same thing about me.

"Good morning," I said cordially as I took the cup he held out. "Thank you."

"You didn't sleep well," he observed. "Can we talk?"

"Yeah, we can after we get the girls to school. We are going to hash this out today." Seth nodded, and we drank our coffee in silence until the girls came down.

Bree came down first and paused in the doorway, eyeing both of us.

"Good morning, honey. Can we talk about Charlie?" I asked. "You and Ella's feelings are really important to me, and I need to know why this is upsetting you."

I sat down at the table and motioned for her to join me. Bree sat down and folded her arms. "I just can't believe you had a baby with someone other than Dad."

Seth joined us at the table. "It was a long time ago, before I ever knew your Mother. So, you can't be mad at her for that. We didn't even know each other then."

"Why did you guys keep this a secret for so long? Why did you lie to us about it?"

I chose my words carefully. "Honey, I never lied to you. It hurt so much to even talk about it, and I just found out who he was now. I had no idea where he lived or even what his name was for twenty years. As soon as I learned about him, I came straight home to tell you. This has been a dream come true for me. I hope that you will choose to be a part of it, too."

Bree thought about it for a moment. "Did he really tell you he wants to meet us?"

I smiled. "More than anything. He said he has always wanted brothers and sisters, and now he can't believe that he has two sisters."

"So, I'm not the oldest anymore," she said.

I smiled. "You're still my oldest daughter. And Ella's big sister. There is nothing better than having a big brother. Will you give him a chance? For me, at least?" I batted my eyes.

Bree rolled her eyes and smirked. "When will we meet him?"

I glanced at Seth. "Soon. I'm not sure when, but soon," I said.

Bree seemed to accept that, and the girls finished getting ready for school. Seth and I appeared normal as we got the kids ready for the bus. Neither Bree nor Ella noticed the dark circles under our eyes, or the new awkwardness that surrounded us.

After texting Elvira to let her know she wasn't needed today, I grabbed a note pad and sat down. Seth eyed it suspiciously. "Wow. Looks like you want to get right to the point. You want to talk divorce already?"

"The sooner we take care of this, the sooner you can be with your girlfriend. I'm assuming she knows about our conversation last night?"

Seth looked out the window and nodded.

"Good. Well, I am assuming that you plan to move in with her…" When Seth didn't respond, I continued. "That means that we will stay here until the house sells. I don't have a job, so I won't be able to maintain a mortgage or utilities. I can live off our savings until it sells, and you can live off your severance."

"And once the house sells, where will you go then?"

I hesitated. "The girls and I are moving back to Minnesota."

"What?" Seth shouted as he slammed his fist on the table, making me jump. "You are going to punish the girls and take them away from me?"

"I am not punishing them at all. They loved Minnesota, and they have more family there than they do here. What am I supposed to do, move our kids into some run-down apartment in the projects while I go and get a fourteen dollar an hour job? Sure, when we sell the house, the vehicles and cash in our stocks, we will have a decent amount of money, but that's not going to last forever. And since neither of us work, our money will bleed dry fast. Plus, there is child support and alimony to think about."

Seth shook his head. "You're out to get me. You want to take everything I have. Most importantly, you want to take my girls."

"That's not true. I will take fifty percent of everything we have. We built this life together. Right now, you will be looking for a job, and when you aren't working you will be following Asia to her movie sets.

Do you think she is going to want you to drag the girls along each time you go and see her? They have school. They need stability. You are a wonderful father and I would never keep them from you. You can visit any time you want."

"Where are you going to live?"

"We will stay at Nana's cabin, for the time being. The girls can have their own room and I will sleep on the couch. I can work on the farm in exchange for rent and live off child support and alimony. Brandon needs the help anyways, and the girls love the farm. You can visit as much as you want, and I can stay in Brandon and Charlotte's house when you do. The girls can stay with you during long holidays and summer breaks. They can Face Time you every day."

"Is this about Charlie? You're going to move our girls so you can be closer to him?"

I laughed in his face. "You need to remember that this is about you, and you no longer want to be married. But yes, I have lived twenty years without my son, and I don't have to do that anymore. Now, all my kids can be closer and can get to know each other. What else can you ask of me? To live here while you jet off with your girlfriend? You know that's not fair."

"I know it's not fair. I just didn't think you would want to move *my* girls a world away from the only life they've ever known."

"They know Chokecherry farm. I can promise you that *our* girls will have a better life on that farm than I ever did."

"Did Brandon okay this already?"

"He's my brother. I don't even need to ask."

***

Just to be sure, I called the farm and got Charlotte. Although she was sad to hear about us, she figured it was coming when Seth and Asia's scandal made national news. She was ecstatic that we chose to return home, and she couldn't wait to tell Brandon.

Had Asia Prescott never entered the picture, I would have happily stayed in my marriage, even after seeing Jason. Saying good-bye to Jason was the hardest thing I'd ever had to do. I had to put my family and my commitments first, even though I never stopped loving him. Would he even want to hear from me now?

Shaking, I sent him a text. *You were right about Seth. My marriage is over.* I hit send and saw the three dots on the bottom of the screen showing he was writing back. I held my breath.

I'm sorry, Macy. He's a fool. When are you coming home?

I smiled. *As soon as my house sells. And school will be over in a week.*

Good. I miss you.

I miss you, too. I wish I wouldn't have ended things so quickly at your place.

Oh me, too. But you are worth the wait. XOXO.

Even though he couldn't see me, I blushed. I was too old for butterflies, yet here they were. *Maybe we can make up for lost time? XOXO*

I had quite a few ideas on how to do that.

So, this was how my story was supposed to end. All of us were going to be okay. I got Jason and Charlie back, and Seth obviously had moved on some time ago. I had never been more excited to end this chapter of my life and start a new one.

CHAPTER 29

JASON

Was there such a thing as redemption? Maybe, just maybe, the universe and the stars had finally aligned. I spent a lifetime fighting for her, and now we had a chance to spend the rest of our lives together.

Nothing was standing in our way this time. There were no devious plots from Elaine, with Howard standing on the sidelines, letting it happen. There was no Seth anymore, either. And soon, there would be no distance between us. Now that I had a reason to be home, it was time to find a new job. Being home wouldn't hurt like it used to.

I didn't know where I would work, and to be honest, it didn't really matter. Maybe I could help Brandon through planting season, and then see what happened from there. My Dad always said to never quit a job without having another one lined up. Well, for the first time in my life, I didn't have a backup plan, and I didn't need one.

I needed to hurry home to be with Macy. My heart skipped a beat just thinking about her. It was our time now, and I wasn't about to let that slip away. I

234

pushed on the gas pedal a little harder. It was now or never.

CHAPTER 30
MACY

We put the house on the market the next week, and it sold in less than twenty-four hours. The buyers accepted the asking price, so no negotiations were needed. Neither of us were prepared to start the daunting task of packing and moving so soon, but since Seth was unemployed, we started right away.

We sold what we could, argued over several items, and I rented a U-Haul to pack the belongings we needed. I took the girls' beds and dressers, as well as one of the living room furniture sets. I donated most of my dress clothes to charity as they were not appropriate for life on Chokecherry farm. The U-Haul filled up fast, and there was no way that all of this would fit into Nana's little cabin. These things were important to us, and there were some things I wasn't willing to part with.

Bree and Ella were devastated by our news. Seth and I told them together, and we held them as they cried. They had so many questions, but mostly they wanted to know why we couldn't work things out. A classmate of Bree's had asked how she felt about her

Dad dating an actress, so Bree looked it up online and saw the pictures plastered all over the Internet. She was furious and she refused to speak to either one of us.

Seth had been staying with Asia ever since that first night I was home. He waited until after the girls went to sleep, and he showed up right before the girls woke up. There were dark circles under his eyes, and he had lost some weight. But I didn't care anymore.

After another exhausting day of packing and managing the girls' emotions, I fell into bed and called Jason.

He picked up on the first ring. "I was just thinking about you. How's it going over there?"

"Not great," I admitted. "The girls are mad at us and we are at each other's throats with all of this packing and moving. I just want this to be over with."

"It's almost done. You got this. When are you heading back here?"

"The last day of school is Thursday. I think closing is Friday. So, we will leave either Friday or Saturday. Brandon found someone to do chores for him. He is going to fly down here Thursday and then take off with the U-Haul right away."

"Would you like to come over for dinner? Whenever you get back, I mean."

"Jason McNally, are you asking me on a date?" I teased.

"You're damn right I am. This time, there is no one to stop us."

***

Elvira came over on the girls' last day of school. Bree and Ella made Elvira cards and we bought her a bouquet of flowers. She cried and hugged us tightly, and since she was speaking in Spanish, none of us understood a word she said. "Por que," she repeated. Seth and I had tears in our eyes when she left.

Brandon arrived by Thursday. He shook Seth's hand when he came in, and then he did his best to ignore him the rest of his visit. He stayed for supper, and then he got on the road. He wanted to be back in Minnesota by Saturday.

Seth took the girls to a movie for their last night, leaving me in an empty house for the last time. I put everything I had into this home. I painted, decorated, and loved every minute. I was going to miss this house immensely.

I sent Jason a text. *This is getting hard. My house is so empty.*

He texted back right away. *I'm sorry. You can do this.*

I know. Thank you for being there for me.

I'm always here for you. I can't wait to see you again.

XOXO .

XOXO, he responded.

                        ***

I was just about to walk into our closing appointment when the phone rang. It was Charlie.

"You guys go on in. I'll be right there," I said, picking up the line. "Hey, Charlie."

There was silence.

"Charlie?"

"Macy, something happened. Something bad."

I felt a chill go through my body. "What happened? Are you okay?"

"It's…Jason. His Dad just called from Arizona. He didn't have your number."

"What's wrong?"

"He...he got into an accident last night. It's bad. Really, really bad."

"What? Wait. How bad?" Charlie didn't answer. "Charlie, how bad is it?"

"Macy, I'm so sorry. He... he didn't make it."

My knees buckled and I fell to the ground. "Are you sure? What happened?" I whispered. A lump formed in the back of my throat. *Please, God, don't let this be true. This can't be.*

"I'm sure. They think that he fell asleep driving. There were no brake marks anywhere and he veered right off the highway. God, I just met him...and now he's gone."

I let Charlie's words sink in. How could this be? I was just getting him back and now I lost him all over again. But this time, I lost him forever.

***

I sat in my parked car for a long time, staring at the blue house with sparkling white shutters. From the outside, nothing looked amiss. The small yard was tidy, with a few shrubs around the front steps and multi-colored tulips down the sidewalk.

But there were two people inside that house who were hurting just as bad as me. Maybe I should have called before I came. I considered it, I really did, but I didn't want them to tell me no. This was something I had to do.

I wiped my sweaty palms on my pants and got out of the car, stretching my stiff, aching body in the oppressive heat. I paused for a moment and contemplated getting back in my car and driving away. *I can't do this.* I opened the car door to get back in when I heard a soft voice call out.

"Wait. Don't go."

I glanced up. A woman was standing on the front steps. Closing the car door again, I slowly walked up to the house.

"You must be Macy?" she asked. I swallowed the lump in my throat and nodded. She smiled at me warmly. "Come inside. We've been waiting for you."

I followed her and immediately felt the welcoming blast of cool air. She led me through the living room and into the kitchen. Silently, she motioned for me to sit at the table while she poured us both a cup of coffee.

"How did you know it was me?" I asked when she sat down.

She smiled. "I would love to say that I just knew, but that would be a lie. Charlie called and gave us a heads up. He was worried about you driving all the way here from Minnesota. That must have been quite a trip." When I shrugged, she continued. "Martin is out running some errands. He should be back anytime. He would like to meet you, too."

"Mrs. McNally, I came to tell you that I am so sorry for your loss."

"Call me Loretta," she patted my hand. "And I am sorry for your loss too, dear. I know he meant a great deal to you." I stared down at my coffee cup and nodded, too upset to say anything else.

"You know, it's a shame that we are just meeting for the first time," Loretta continued. "I remember how shocked I was to hear that you were pregnant, but how excited I was that you two were coming to see us. This visit has been twenty years in the making."

Suddenly the floodgates opened. "I'm sorry…I was coming to pay my respects to you…and now look at me. I'm such a mess. It's just…it's just not fair. It took a whole lifetime for us to finally find each other again. And now he's gone. I didn't even get to say goodbye."

Loretta pulled her chair over and gave me a hug.

"I know, dear. I know." When my cries subsided into hiccups, she continued. "Macy, you need to know that I have never seen my son as happy as he was when he was with you. I watched helplessly as he tortured himself trying to find you and Charlie for so many years. And when he finally found you again, well, it was a dream come true for him."

"It was for me too. I never stopped loving him," I said.

"I know. And it gives me such peace knowing how happy he was. He got his son back. He got you back. He had everything he had ever wanted, even though it was for such a short time. He was no longer haunted by his past. You and Charlie were the best thing that ever could have happened to him. And I will forever be thankful for that."

"That means so much to me, thank you," I said.

"Am I interrupting?" a voice said from the entryway.

Loretta smiled. "Not at all, dear. Macy, this is my husband, Martin. Martin, this is Macy." I stood up and offered my hand. He opened his arms and gave me a big hug instead.

"Thank you for dropping by," he said huskily. "It means a great deal to us."

"Thank you for seeing me, even though I came unannounced. I wanted to drop by and tell you how sorry I am," I said again.

"Would you like to stay for dinner, dear?" Loretta asked as she got Martin a cup of coffee.

I smiled. "I'd like that very much."

Martin sat down at the table. "We had a feeling you would be dropping by. And then Charlie called us to let us know that you were on your way. Loretta and I have been talking and there are a few things we would like to talk to you about, now that you are here," Martin said, folding his hands together in his lap.

"Anything," I said.

Loretta and Martin looked at each other. "My parents owned the house on Birch Lake," Martin said. "When they passed away, Jason inherited it. We would like to keep it in the family, so we were wondering how you would feel if we gave it to Charlie."

"What you choose to do with it is none of my business," I said quickly, holding both of my palms up. "I shouldn't have any say in where it goes."

Martin nodded. "Okay, it's settled then. We will talk to Charlie about it and see if he is interested in it."

Loretta looked at Martin. "Should we bring up the other thing?" Martin went into another room.

"The other thing?" I asked.

Martin appeared a moment later and sat back down, placing a large metal object on the table. I gasped. It was Jason's urn.

"Jason always said he didn't want a funeral, or anyone to make any sort of fuss when he died. So, we respected his wishes, and had him cremated. After much prayer and reflection, we realized that his home was never here in Arizona. His life has been and will always be in Minnesota," Martin said.

"Martin and I would like you to have his urn. Perhaps you have somewhere special where you could spread his ashes?" Loretta gave a knowing smile.

My fingers ran over the cold metal urn as I swallowed another lump in my throat. "I know the perfect place."

EPILOGUE

The girls' suitcases were packed and ready to go. Now that school was out, they were going to spend a month with Seth in Los Angeles. The girls were looking forward to it, and I needed the break.

Seth found another job in Los Angeles, but this time with life estates and living wills. While he would admit it was not as exciting as being a high-profile divorce lawyer, it paid the bills and kept him out of trouble. Asia and Seth are no longer together. I wouldn't know if he was seeing anyone now, and it would never cross my mind to ask. All I cared about was his relationship with our daughters, and I was impressed with how much he stayed in their lives. They spent every long break with him this past year, and they Face Time him almost every day.

Charlie and the girls had become inseparable. He stopped over as often as he could, and we often met him in Saint Cloud for dinner or a movie. We even spent a weekend at his parent's place in Fargo. Uncle Doug and Auntie Courtney, as the girls call them, were gracious enough to include us in their family, and they have never made me feel anything other than family. I feel like I've known them forever. They are beautiful people, and Charlie is so lucky to have them in his life.

We all are.

While we were in Fargo, we met Heather and her beautiful family. She was happier than ever and lived a chaotic and busy life. She has been my rock this last year, just as she was when I was in the convent. I am thankful that our relationship picked right back up where we left off.

I've run into Leah several times over the past year, and we are getting to the point of being more than cordial. She's still clean and working hard to repair the damaged relationships with her children. I was proud of her, and I tell her that every time I see her. While I didn't go out of my way to avoid her, I also haven't quite invited her in. Some walls take a long time to come down.

Life on the farm has been different. It took the girls less than a minute to adjust, and they loved to ride their bikes and climb on hay bales. I got them up and ready for school and would send them over to Charlotte's while I started the morning milking. I did the afternoon milkings, and then I was there with the girls when they got home from school. We usually headed over to Brandon and Charlotte's for supper, and after I did the dishes and cleaned the kitchen, we headed home to do homework. With Charlotte expecting their fifth baby any day, I knew I was going to be needed more than ever.

The past year tested my strength and courage more than any other year. With Martin and Loretta's permission, I spread Jason's ashes at Willow's Pond. I spread some in the pond, around the Willow trees, bench, and pasture. And what remained was spread over where Jason parked and hid his truck for so many months. It was the spot we confirmed our pregnancy, and the spot where he held me in his arms while we planned out our life together. A year later, the pond was still where I felt the most serene. Each day I would sneak away for a few minutes, just to sit on the wooden bench. I could feel the breeze brush against my face, and I no longer felt so alone. When I closed my eyes, I could feel Jason wrapping his arms around me.

"Hey, babe," I whispered. Although he doesn't answer, I know he's there. He was always there. His presence was everywhere on Chokecherry. I could *feel* him. And I always would.

Thank you for reading Chokecherry Drive. I hope you enjoyed reading it as much as I enjoyed writing it. Please leave a review on Amazon.

Follow me on Facebook—
www.FaceBook.com/Author Layla Reed.

Made in the USA
San Bernardino, CA
30 November 2019

60670307R00153